Trippin'

Also by
Michelle Buckley

Bulletproof Soul

Trippin'

Michelle Buckley

www.urbanbooks.net

Urban Books
1199 Straight Path
West Babylon, NY 11704

ISBN-13: 978-1-60162-061-3
ISBN-10: 1-60162-061-6

First Trade Paperback Printing: July 2006
First Mass Market Paperback Printing: May 2008
Printed in the United States of America

10   9   8   7   6   5   4   3   2   1

*This is a work of fiction. Any references or similarities to ac-
tual events, real people, living, or dead, or to real locales are
intended to give the novel a sense of reality. Any similarity in
other names, characters, places, and incidents is entirely coin-
cidental.*

Submit Wholesale Order to:
Kensington Publishing Corp.
C/O Penguin Group (USA) Inc.
Attention: Order Processing
405 Murray Hill Parkway
East Rutherford, NJ 07073-2316
Phone: 1-800-526-0275
Fax: 1-800-227-9604

Acknowledgments

If you're looking for *Bulletproof Soul II*, you aren't going to find it here.

My second novel, *Trippin'* is a very different tale. I think as a writer, your goals should always be to connect with readers and touch their hearts and look for new challenges as you develop your craft. Hopefully, I've accomplished all of the above and will affect readers profoundly with my sexy, new novel. Not only am I writing from a darker place, but I've also taken up the challenge of writing for 7 main characters (yes, it's as hard as it sounds!)

While this is a very different read from *Bulletproof Soul*, I hope you'll enjoy it all the same. This book wouldn't be possible were it not for some key supporters. I'd like to first give glory to God for allowing me to once again fulfill my dream of being a writer. I'd also like to thank my parents, Myrna and Stanley Buckley—who are my two biggest fans—and my two biggest booksellers! Also, much thanks to my aunt Georgette Session, who single-handedly took Dallas, Texas by storm promoting my first book!

Much love to my other kinfolk who have supported me along my journey, including: my grandmother, Gertrude Spurgeon, Stan, Kristen and

Faith Buckley, R.A. and Reggie Session, Maple Session, Nicole and Jay McIlveen, Erma Washington and Belle Doxey, Trudy Spurgeon, Carol and Ida Eubanks, Lue Calhoun, Bob and Pam Lynch, Gloria and Charles Saunders, Marguerite and Linda Waller, Barbara and Jessica Garrett, Robin and Curtis Drapeau, Faye and Flip Smith, Julia Buckley, Tonya and Carl Bass, Kevin and Herman Buckley, Deann King, Elizabeth Hubbard, Penny Barnes, Anna Mae Woods, Moses Woods, George Woods, Jackie Woods and the entire Woods family.

Thanks also to long-time friends and associates Deborah Maxwell, Roz Allen, Vertie Byrd, Edith Knox, the Paynes, the Porters, the Criners, the Bennetts, MC Richardson, Celina Robinson, KU's Marshall Jackson and the congregation of St. Luke Church of God in Christ.

To Carl Weber, my publisher and mentor . . . thank you for your patience. To author, Roy Glenn and his wife, Arvita Glenn, thank your for your encouragement, and to my editor, Martha Weber, your guidance as always was tremendous!

Finally, I'd like to thank book clubs, fellow writers, bloggers and media personalities who supported me, including: Black Expressions.com, Gwen and Willie Richardson, owners of Cushcity.com, Kansas City Girlfriends Book Club, Tanisha Webb, the Kansas City Mahogany Book Club, Black Images, Tee C. Royal, Maxine Thompson, George Cook, Nickolas Alexander, Tish Williams, Crystal Gamble (Nardsbaby), Shay Cousar, LaShaunda C. Hoffman, Tommi Patterson, the Kansas City Soul Book Club, Mahogany Interpretations Book Club, the Only One Stroke Away online book club, People Who Love Good Books, Sormag.com,

KPRS/KPRT Radio, Sean Tyler, Julee Jonez, Shawn Edwards, Monica Nightengale, The Kansas City Star's Steve Penn and Lisa Guitterez, 107.9 JAMZ-Wichita, Kan., Jeff Primos of fountaincity.com, Ken Lumpkins of kcsoul. com, Annie Work at Urban News, Bonita Gooch at the Community Voice, the University of Kansas Black Alumni Association, the Kansas City Missouri and Mid-Continent Public Libraries, authors Brandon Massey, Elaine Flowers, Tiffani Palmer, Rose Jackson-Beavers, Shandra Love, Stacy-Deanne, Sheila Goss, Cydney Rex, Donna Hill, Monica Jackson, Trista Russell, Alisha Yvonne, Ashley JaQuavis, Dwayne Joseph, LaTonya Y. Williams, Toschia Moffett, White Chocolate and the entire Urban Books family.

If you've supported me and you do not find your name here, please know that's merely a function of limited space . . . not of limited gratitude.

To learn more about me or to offer feedback on my work, visit me online anytime at michelle buckleyblog.blogspot.com or michellebuckley.com. You can also drop me an e-mail anytime you'd like at prgalkc@hotmail.com.

God bless you all, thanks for the support and happy reading.

"The journey is the reward."
~ Taoist Proverb

THE BEGINNING OF THE END

"Whitney Houston only got it half right: Crack ain't all that's whack—so is life." That's what an old friend once told him before dying. Why he was thinking about that now as he lay floating in a pool face down, inhaling water and blood into his lungs, ass saluting the sky, he didn't exactly know. Maybe it was because of the simple fact that he, like Whitney, had issues.

His wife used to always tell him that, and he would always respond, "We all got issues—some folks are just better at hiding them than others."

Angie Stone's joint, "Mad Issues," could have been his theme song. He had plenty of issues, and like most frontin' Negroes who try to come across as more than they are, he was good at hiding his flaws. He didn't wear that shit on his sleeves the way suburban white kids rock Sean John gear or an inmate rocks his prison number; he kept his issues under cover, under wraps, so much so that everyone who knew him thought he was nearly perfect. If only they knew.

His number one mad issue was that he was a killer. Compared to that, the rest of his issues didn't really seem to matter much. Yeah, he was greedy, when it came to women, money, and material possessions, but all of that took a backseat to being a murderer.

His ass-toe started itching. That wasn't a good sign.

In college, while trying to earn some extra cash, Darryn shoveled snow on campus grounds for his college's landscaping service. As a result of not following severe winter weather guidelines, he got frostbite and had to have the big toe on his left foot amputated. After raising a stink about the possibility of a lawsuit, his company paid him a small settlement.

Too vain to walk around toeless, Darryn used the money to pay for the reconstruction of his big toe. Doctors used some skin from his ass to reconstruct the toe, and while it wasn't the most attractive thing in the world, it did the job. It was a little crazy-looking, but he swore his ass-toe had special powers.

Whenever it itched, it normally signaled two things—it was either a sure sign that he and his wife were going to have fantastic sex, or it was a sign that he was in deep trouble. From the way things were looking, he was betting on the latter.

As he lay floating somewhere between death and semi-consciousness, he knew that neither his ass-toe nor his going through a laundry list of his faults could help him. For him, it was too late. It was over, or at least it would be soon.

He couldn't remember when his world first started turning to crap. All he knew was that once a brother started going downhill; the trip was over fast. And he brought the love of his life down with him fast too—or was it the other way around?

Ambition will do that to you—get you all confused. Ride you fast and hard like a woman that ain't had none for a while, or like an alcoholic fresh off the wagon and dipping in the sauce again.

Personally, he thought the word ambition had received a bad rap.

Without it, a person would go nowhere. They'd stand still, not moving, not living. And hell, inertia killed or at the very least made you stupid, simple, or crazy.

Harriet Tubman freeing slaves . . .

Venus Williams, a tennis menace . . .

Carl Lewis, Michael Johnson, and Shani Davis winning Olympic gold . . .

Shaq and Kobe, ballers extraordinaire . . .

Oprah Winfrey, first black female billionaire . . .

Reuben Studdard, American Idol . . .

Barack Obama, President????

That level of accomplishment and achievement was the result of ambition, pure and simple, not to mention a lot of desire, determination, talent, and hustle—all of that and the hand of God.

He knew there were a lot of things folks could say about him, but accusing him of not having ambition wasn't one of those things.

No matter what it was, he wasn't afraid to go after what he wanted, and he usually got it.

Over the years, he had displayed plenty of ambition: Go to college on scholarship—check; marry the prettiest and smartest chick on campus—check; get a job at a top accounting firm—check.

In fact, his ambition could be considered his number two issue. Perhaps he'd been too ambitious, and that's what led him down his destructive path.

He hated to admit it, but his friend was right.

Life is whack—whether you're on top of the world like he once was or at the bottom like he was now.

Hell, he knew exactly what he'd do differently if only he was given a second chance, if only he could call a do-over. For starters he wouldn't have had anything to do with DAT Club—that's when his problems truly began and when he realized—too late—an obvious truth:

Real recognizes real . . .

Game recognizes game . . .

Freaks recognize freaks, and

Killers recognize killers.

MADETRA

Doctor Madetra Price cringed as she neared the frosted glass door that read *3 Weiss Men.* "Yeah, and one dumb ass," Mad mumbled under her breath as she entered the practice of African-American psychiatrist, E'an Shaw, and his three partners.

E'an Shaw—said dumb ass—was the only shrink in an otherwise all-Jewish family medicine practice made up of three brothers—Jon, Ben, and Abraham Weiss. The brothers started the practice years ago, out of a desire to help the poor, but they were so good, even rich whites traveled to the hood to be treated by them. Those rich whites were the patients who kept the bills paid, not the Medicare and Medicaid patients that Madetra, a Kansas City family practitioner, treated.

The Weiss brothers' upscale clientele definitely paid for her black patients' care, and because of that well-heeled clientele, the doctors had hired special security to watch over their elite clients' vehicles and bodies.

Madetra was lucky. She had just gotten out of medical school and wanted to start her practice in the neighborhood she grew up in, when she'd stumbled upon the Weiss brothers at a professional conference. Luckily, the Weiss brothers had some extra space and were willing to rent it to her cheap. Not only was rent cheap, but for a few years, Mad's patients benefited from the top-rate security too, at no cost to her. Apparently that was all about to change.

Mad shook her head as she re-read the letter. One phrase in particular stood out—$600 a month for shared upgraded security.

WTF?

Mad didn't have that kind of money! Between paying off her school loans, paying her malpractice insurance, not to mention rent, and the wages and benefits for the new receptionist they'd just hired but didn't need, she was finding it harder and harder to break even, let alone turn a profit. She was already working 60 hours a week, but the more she worked, the more her expenses increased. The mere thought of all of her expenses made her start to hyperventilate.

As she stopped in her tracks to catch her breath, her least favorite person in the world appeared in front of her from out of nowhere.

E'an Shaw greeted her in his typical obnoxious fashion. "Hey, Killer Bod. What's up?"

A smart-as-a-whip Harvard Medical School grad, E'an was ruggedly handsome, not drop-dead, model gorgeous, and exuded unshakeable self-assurance and confidence. On paper and at first glance, he seemed to be the total package. He was dark, over six feet tall, had a nice, stocky build, small retro Afro, and was stylish, young, attractive, and, worse yet, knew it.

"E'an, I am a doctor . . . same as you. You can't just talk to me any kind of way. I think I've earned your respect," Mad said, exasperated.

"Okay, *Doctor* Killer Bod, what up?" A smile spread across his face.

The frown clouding Mad's features somewhat obscured her attractiveness. "Why do you call me that?" Madetra asked. His reference to her body made her painfully aware of the few extra pounds she'd gained over the last few months.

She now weighed about 150 pounds and had gone up to a size 14. That made her self-conscious, and it showed in her face and the way she carried herself.

Short, dark-skinned, and deep-dimpled, Madetra had a heart of gold. She wore her naturally long hair straight, with just a hint of curl at the ends. In many people's eyes—E'an included among the group—Madetra was the perfect woman.

"Because you have one hell of a body."

"You're a pig. Are any of the Weiss brothers here? I need to talk to them about my security bill and the new receptionist that's been hired."

"They are all out to lunch. And besides, I sent that bill. What's there to talk about? You need to chip in for your fifth of the security costs starting next month, period; we can no longer carry you."

"I don't happen to have an extra $600 just lay-ing around, E'an. Do we really need to even up-grade our security?"

"This ain't even up for discussion, Killer Bod—

excuse me—*Doctor* Killer Bod. We warned you this might be a possibility at our last staff meeting. I've got a patient waiting on me, so I have to go."

Mad eyed him with disgust as he started to walk off.

"And, oh yeah," he said turning around, "I heard about your travel club from Gerald the last time he was in here doing massages. I guess I'll be seeing you at tomorrow night's meeting. Peace and a bottle of hair grease." He winked and proceeded down the hall.

"Jerk!" Madetra mumbled under her breath.

E'an had been the bane of her existence for the last two years, ever since she chose to rent space from the Weiss Men and open a practice in their building.

From what Madetra had seen and heard over the years, he was good and compassionate with his patients but a total jerk when it came to everyone else, particularly women.

He'd hit on Madetra every day for the past two years. With time, as her rejection got more brutal, so did his come-ons.

More than once she thought about telling her husband, eager to have him give the good doctor a beat-down, but she couldn't risk totally alienating E'an, because as expensive as it was to rent space from the Weiss Men, she knew it would be more expensive to have a practice elsewhere in the city. So for the most part, she just took his abuse and suffered in silence. She hoped that eventually he would get tired and just stop.

E'an wasn't the first man to sexually harass her. A boss of hers in college sexually harassed the hell out of her. He told her he didn't care if she reported him or not. He said being alone with her for just one night would make it all worth it. Her boss had made up excuses to keep her late after work, and then he would tell her dirty jokes and make suggestive remarks.

Once, she swore he was masturbating under his desk while doing her employee review. She documented everything. Luckily, he was stupid enough to hit on her with others around. His harassment cost the pizza joint he was the manager of an undisclosed amount of money, and it cost him his wife! Shortly after he was fired, Madetra had his job!

Her situation with E'an was much more precarious, or so she thought. His mere presence made her skin crawl. The way he undressed her with his eyes, made her nervous and uncomfortable. She managed to cut interaction down to as little as possible, but E'an still managed to get to her. And now he was going to be in her travel club? The thought made her sick to her stomach. She prayed he was kidding but had no intentions of stopping him if he wasn't. She desperately needed the space in the Weiss men's building for her practice and she had to stay on their business manager's good side.

"E'an, I wasn't done," she yelled, just as he was rounding the corner. She jogged to him, observing his eyes on her chest the whole time. She did her best to keep her growing anger in check. "I also need to talk to you about the new receptionist you hired; I don't think it's a good fit," she whispered under her breath as they stood only feet away from the reception area.

"What? You don't like Thalia?" E'an asked in a louder than necessary tone.

Mad yanked him down the hall by his arm. "Shhhhh! Be quiet, E'an!"

It was a well-known fact that Madetra considered Thalia Dawnn a joke! Her dark, ashen skin was the color of mud. Not that anyone knew what color she really was because every time she appeared in public, she was fully made-up—eyes, mouth, cheeks, the works! Mad wondered how she'd look without makeup. *Probably really scary!*

Excessive-perfume-wearing, bug-eyed, weave-flipping, ghetto-fabulous gold digger—that was Thalia to a T! At least that's what Madetra had heard from folks who knew of her. From what Madetra had learned, Thalia was always trying to give the appearance of having class but always fell far short. Mad wondered how she could afford her designer clothes, fancy purses, expensive shoes, high-class perfume, and other fancy items, considering she was nothing but a glorified secretarial temp. Hell, Madetra was a doctor and wasn't rolling like that, but then again she didn't use men for money and she didn't have sex with anyone and everyone.

Not only was Thalia a slut, but she was also the angriest black female Mad had ever seen. She didn't have a true compassionate bone in her body. That came across every time her interaction with a patient went above and beyond having to say, "Please sign in and take a seat." Although she pretended to be nice and sensitive, she really wasn't. She was one of the few people that you could say deserved all the bad that happened to her in her life. In her case, karma was no joke.

Madetra had learned through the grapevine

that Thalia had destroyed more than a few mar-
riages.

And as karma would dictate, at 33, no one was
scrambling to marry her. From what Mad could
see, the reasons were obvious—she was oppor-
tunistic, and had an ugly spirit and a jealous heart.

"I don't want Thalia as our receptionist. Using
the office manager as our receptionist was working
out just fine."

"We needed to free up Natalie's time. Thalia has
just been on the job a few weeks. Give her time;
she'll get the hang of things. She'll grow on you.
Besides, you have no choice but to accept her."

"Why her? Can she even do the job? I've heard
from friends and my sister Kay that she's been let
go from every secretarial job she's ever had. She
has no real skills, too much attitude, and she's not
a team player. You name the complaint, I've heard
it about her, or I've seen it for myself these last two
weeks. She's been mostly unemployed the past two
years. She's been working sporadically as a temp.
How did she even get a job here at the clinic? Huh
E'an? How?"

"I don't know what you're talking about. She
comes to us with glowing references. Nobody else
has a problem with her, including the Weiss men,
so why don't you just chill out and let her do her
job?"

"The Weiss men don't have a problem with her
because they spend all day with patients and don't
know what's really going on in the reception area.
Plus, I'm sure you're probably covering like crazy
for her. What did you do? Where did you find her?
Did you pick her up at some club?"

"Actually, it was a restaurant-bar," E'an answered smugly.

"Nice. Does she even have a completed application or references on file? Don't even bother answering that. I can tell the answer from your expression. I don't like having her around. Her whole aura is whack. You know how some people can walk in a room and brighten it up? She walks in and darkens a room. Her aura is so black and bleak; that's the last thing we need in reception. We need a ray of sunshine at the front desk. She's more like a P-O-D—a Princess of Darkness, Satan."

"Well, if it helps any, the Princess of Darkness cums like sunshine. When she has an orgasm, she lights up the room . . . just like I imagine you do."

"Believe it or not, I'd prefer our patients not know how she cums. I should have known you were sleeping with her!"

"Believe me, there ain't no sleeping going on. And between you and me, she thinks that because I gave her a little job here she's running things, but truly she's not. Tricks like her are a dime a dozen. You, on the other hand . . . if you wanted to dump your zero husband and take a ride with, I mean, *on* me, the world could be yours."

"If you're so taken by me, E'an, fire her." Madetra batted her eyes and gently brushed his hand.

She took a step back after a wave of electricity ran through his body and back into her own that both surprised and disgusted her.

"No can do. Satan, the P-O-D, the Princess of Darkness, Thalia—whatever you want to call her— is staying, period. I promised her a job, and I'm nothing, if not a man of my word."

"Okay, fine! Do business with the devil. Just tell me one thing—does Satan take dictation?"

"No, but she can sure take this nine inches, without any problems." E'an laughed as he grabbed his crotch.

"E'an, you're a pig, not to mention a son of a bitch," Mad told him before walking away.

"The most important trip you may take in life is meeting people halfway."
~ Henry Boye

E'AN

"**S**he needs to cut the bull. She wants me," Dr. E'an Shaw said aloud as he continued to walk to his office.

He loved being as perverse as possible with Madetra Price. The Killer Bod comments threw her over the edge every time, and that tickled him to no end. He made sure that he only harassed her when no one was around. That way, if he were ever sued, it would be her word against his. He knew she only took the abuse because she was between a rock and a hard place—her practice was relatively new, and she couldn't afford to rent space anywhere else in the city. Plus, she grew up in the area and wanted to give back to her community. If she hadn't had such a big heart and wasn't so desperate, E'an was sure she would have sued his behind long ago.

He smiled inwardly as he relived the look of pure terror that crossed her face when he mentioned that he'd be at her travel club meeting. He'd have to thank Gerald for telling him about it.

The thought of joining a travel club, particularly Madetra's, intrigued E'an. Lord knows, he needed a vacation, and without being forced to take one, he'd never take any time off. Originally, he was only kidding about attending her travel club meeting, but after her reaction, he knew he had to be there. He chuckled aloud at the thought. If he showed up, she'd have a fit . . . if he were lucky.

E'an and Madetra's relationship was the equivalent of an extremely one-sided school-age crush, except instead of pulling her pigtails, he got on her nerves any way he could. She returned his overtures with total disdain, which only fueled his desire for her even more. So what if the good doctor hated him now? That would all change. Eventually. Hopefully.

She was used to being a pampered, spoiled, praised, cajoled princess. He'd watched her closely in professional settings—at American Medical Association meetings, at meetings with the board, and at staff meetings. The men who treated her like a queen got eaten for lunch. She had no respect for them and wrapped them around her fingers. Well, he wasn't going out like that.

E'an entered his office—a sterile psychiatric sanctuary of pastel wood and muted tones—and snapped himself out of his Madetra Price fantasy.

The fact that E'an was a psychiatrist was no accident. He had learned a long time ago that everyone had a little crazy in them; it was just harder to detect in some people than others. He'd been dealing with crazies all his life, which pretty much included every woman he'd ever dated as well as his crazy, obsessive-compulsive, alcoholic mother.

Growing up, it had been just the two of them. His father disappeared when he was really young. He'd heard stories from his mother ranging from his father left to be with his other family to he left to join some super-secretive government agency. The more drunk his mother was, the more entertaining the stories were about why his father left them.

By the time he was in junior high, E'an got tired of all the stories. He gave up trying to figure out what was really the truth because he no longer cared.

When she wasn't drunk off her behind, his mother was a neat freak. To this day, he could vividly remember how at least once a week when he was younger, she would awaken him to clean dishes—literally every dish in the house—just because she found one spot on a glass, saucer, or plate. He hated her for that and every other obsessive-compulsive thing she ever did or made him do. He also hated her for all the times she embarrassed him while she was drunk. This included the time she fought the mailman in their front yard because he failed to deliver a certain catalog on a certain day and the day she came to his school in her robe—and not much else—so that he could open a jar of jelly for her.

When he turned eighteen, needless to say, he couldn't get away from his mother's home fast enough. He moved out to California, and put himself through college and eventually got into Harvard Medical School.

E'an hadn't had contact with his mother since

he'd left home at eighteen. He didn't know if she was still alive, and he didn't care. She had never been close to anyone in her family, and he knew of no relatives, so he really had no way of finding out about his mother, nor did he want to.

E'an stared at his one o'clock patient and smiled. *Poor, crazy, delusional Mr. Poole.*

"If you can't beat 'em, join 'em," E'an mumbled under his breath. "How are you today, Mr. Poole?"

Before Mr. Poole could answer, E'an dropped to his hands and knees and kicked his feet up against the wall so that he was standing on his head—just like Mr. Poole.

And then their session began.

KAYLANTRA

The average woman takes 27 minutes to have an orgasm.

As she was staring into her webcam, trying to have an orgasm of her own, Kaylantra tried to remember where she'd read that—*Cosmo, Jane, Honey, Essence, Today's Black Woman, Smooth, King, Maxim, Stuff*—heck, she couldn't remember.

Thank God, it didn't take her that long; she didn't have that kind of time. It would be bad for business. *Shoot, in 27 minutes, she could have four orgasms, but that came—no pun intended—with practice.*

Twenty-nine-year-old Kaylantra Ellis had been bumping and grinding, moaning and groaning, shaking and quaking in front of the camera for a while. She knew early on, she wasn't nearly as book smart as some women, so she learned, at a young age, to use what assets she *did* have to make money.

She started her webcam site—alwayshot&ready. com—six months ago. She charged a fee of $19.95

per visit and usually had 100 visitors a week. That didn't include what she charged for chats afterwards when she took requests. (That was an additional $19.95 per hour, and she tried to draw the chats out for as long as she could, usually two hours.) It also didn't include the $1.99 she charged for nude picture downloads. In a given week, she could easily make up to $5,000 online. Who knew pleasuring oneself for the entertainment of strangers could be so lucrative?

A friend that she worked with at the strip club down in the cut, HOTGIRLZ, had hipped her to the sexual happenings on the Net, and just like the prospectors who'd benefited from the early days of the gold rush, Kay was experiencing a rush of her own and loving it! Feeling the heat between her legs rise as she touched herself, she smiled impishly for the camera and thought of him, the man she always thought of before she climaxed— the fine light-skinned brother who was a regular on her favorite soap opera, *The Young and the Restless*.

She loved to fantasize about him touching her most intimate parts. He was the man she had named all her sex toys after, including her favorite, spiky 8-inch dildo. She knew it was silly, but like George Foreman, who'd named all his kids George, she felt compelled to name all her toys after him— items 1 through 18.

She let her mind guide her into the wonderful world of mental stimulation. She anticipated the spasm that would rock her as she pictured his sturdy, manly hands deeply caressing her thighs and then her backside, dancing across her womanly curves, touching her, stroking her, loving her.

She imagined him massaging her best features—
her breasts—and as her moans grew deeper and
perspiration began to dot her unblemished skin,
she visualized him sliding his fingers inside the wet
slit of her bald, pierced, feminine mound. She felt
like silk ribbon unfurling. In her mind, he was
there with her caressing her and kissing her until
the last drop of the liquid remnant of her passion
flowed down her thighs.

Twenty-seven minutes, my behind, she thought.
When she was done, she mentally prepared herself
for the chat, her least favorite part of the evening.

"You seemed extra lubricated," Killthekitty typed.

"I came at the same time you did, just like always,"
her horny, long-time female regular, Sayno2mono
gamy wrote.

"So did I," typed Bigslickrick.

"Dildo, I mean ditto," Oversyxed typed.

Kay rolled her eyes as she read their comments.
She wasn't in the mood for chatting . . . until
something special caught her eye.

*"Instead of just seeing your body, tonight I saw your
soul,"* SoulViewer typed.

Kay sensed that the person who typed this wasn't
the normal, run-of-the-mill pervert who usually visited her site. Whoever it was that was seeing her soul
was special and made her feel special too.

"I'm flattered," she responded.

*"Good. Then my job here is done. I am so drawn to
you. You're special, magical. YOU ARE MAGIC. You're
made of magic and you have tiny magic rays emitting
from that bangin' magic body of yours. In the words of
the mighty Vince Vaughn, it's like you're stuffed with
Elvis dust."*

Kay laughed. How did SoulViewer know that

Vince Vaughn, the hyper thespian from some of her favorite movies like *Swingers, Made,* and *Old School,* was one of her favorite comedic actors?

Drawn in by the stranger's comments, Kay turned all of her attention to her newfound friend, and the two chatted pretty much all night, ignoring everyone else.

Hours later, as she tumbled into bed, Kay felt bad about all the complaints she had received about her chatting all night long with one man. To make up for her behavior, she knew the next time she was in front of her webcam, she would have to put on an extra special show.

With any luck, she hoped SoulViewer would be watching.

"Not all those who wander are lost."
~ J. R. R. Tolkien Lord of the Rings

FINESSE

"Good evening, Kansas City. I'm Finesse Brown, here, with your five-minute news update."

"Dang, how fine am I?" the vain and arrogant tv anchor asked himself as he read aloud a story about a six-year-old missing boy. "I'm still fine as wine, apparently. Look at the way my producer is grinning from ear to ear. Dang! That girl still wants me! Maybe I'll have pity on her tonight and break her off a little something that she can really smile about," he almost said aloud.

"And now, here's Rex Anderson with sports," Finesse said, barely able to interrupt his self-absorbed thoughts.

As Rex did his standard sports shtick, Finesse continued to bask in his thoughts. *Destanie, you had it going on at one time, in the bed and in your head, but then you got clingy on me. You contracted CBS— Crazy Broad Syndrome.*

"That's it for this news brief. Good night, Kansas City," Finesse said with a fake smile and wink.

When he was done, Destanie Beri—his over-zealous producer, approached the anchor desk. "That was great, Finney."

Channel 55 was a low budget station as far as money spent on sets and salaries, but luckily the talent they had was first-rate, including Destanie and Finesse, who worked the afternoon/evening news shifts at the fifth-ranked station.

"Finney, if you have a moment, I'd like to meet with you to go over the promos and tomorrow's newscast," Destanie said, after the cameras were off and everyone else behind the scenes had left.

He lied. "Can't. Got plans." Then he almost asked her, "Dang, girl! Why are you always playing yourself?"

"Really? What kind of plans?"

"Destanie, don't go there."

"Fine. So am I still going to see you at that travel club meeting tomorrow night? You know we're covering the trips for the news as part of a series."

"I'll be there."

Finesse didn't really like being so mean to her, but sometimes it was called for. He examined himself in the mirror behind her. For a long while, she'd been cramping his style. He was honey-brown, tall and thin, with a baldhead and piercing green eyes. Long considered God's gift to women, Finesse was arrogant and had always known he was destined for greatness.

The fact that he was on television was no sur-prise to anyone, even though he didn't have a journalism degree. He'd managed to work his way from the mailroom to in front of the cameras. From an early age, he considered it his destiny to be seen and he wasn't planning to stop until he hit prime time network news.

Destanie, on the other hand, loved working in mid-city news and had no desire to work for the networks. She, unlike Finesse, had a degree and background in journalism. Channel 55 was her second job as a producer.

She was pretty in an unassuming way, short, and a tad overweight according to her doctor—twenty pounds to be exact.

She had a beautiful face and nice hair, and when she fixed herself up, she looked really hot. The two got together purely by accident. Drinking after newscasts nearly seven months ago, they got really loose and real friendly, and before they knew it, they were rocking it back in one of the editing bays.

Things were good for about six months. But then Finesse got bored, and Destanie got needy. That was three weeks ago.

"You know, Finney, if you don't get a better attitude, I don't know how we're going to work together. I might just have to ask to work with a different anchor," Destanie's whiny voice said, abruptly jolting him out of his remembrances of the past.

"You are truly a hot mess! Don't threaten me. Don't start any nonsense with me on the job! I'll do what I have to do for my assignments, but that doesn't include getting in your drawers."

His crassness made her burst into tears.

"I ain't trying to have an emotional scene up in here, Destanie. Let's keep things strictly professional between us from now on—that's all I'm saying," he told her, softening up a little.

"Forget you! I ain't trying to hear your 'let's-stay-professional' BS!" she yelled at him before exiting the studio.

For the life of him, he could not understand why Destanie just couldn't let go. He had never loved her. He always made sure to never utter those words unless he really meant it.

Hell, he'd only really loved one woman in his life, his first girlfriend in high school—Shawnna Roberts.

Like everyone predicted, the first-love passion Finesse felt for Shawnna eventually folded from the weight of pregnancy, abortion, infidelity, lies, sexually transmitted disease, parental disapproval, and good, old-fashioned teenage insecurity and angst.

Shawnna was a virgin when they first got together, and while no one knew it, so was seventeen-year-old Finesse. Up until that point, Finesse thought he was too good and too fine to be with anybody. During the three years that they were a couple, together they discovered the joy of sex and turned each other out in ways that only first loves could. Like most high-school sweethearts, there was always plenty of drama swarming around the two of them, but when Shawnna got pregnant by Finesse a second time, her family decided it was time to move. They moved her across country, leaving them both to deal with their broken hearts as best they could.

Shawnna turned to food, and the last Finesse heard, she weighed over 300 pounds. Meanwhile, Finesse turned to other women—lots of them. In fact that's how he got his job as a television anchor-man—by sleeping with an associate producer at the station.

He managed to get a job in the station's mail-room when he was twenty-four. He mainly slaved away for three years in the mailroom in the bowels of the station's basement, but once he moved up to become the mailroom supervisor, he got the op-portunity to deliver mail throughout the building.

Being the hustler he was, Finesse took full ad-vantage of those situations by meeting and be-friending every person he came in contact with, particularly the young women. One such friend, Jennifer, a white girl from Kentucky, grew fond of him to the point where they had a standing "date" every Wednesday at noon.

On one particular Wednesday, instead of their usual quickie, Jennifer "borrowed" a newly pressed and cleaned suit from the station's top male an-chor and dressed Finesse in it and insisted that the powers-that-be at the station audition him for a low-level anchor position.

When they scoffed at the idea, Jennifer threat-ened to help him sue the station for racial discrim-ination. That was the first time he'd ever known a white girl to take up for a black man like that, but it certainly wasn't the first or last time a woman would risk everything for him.

In the end, Finney got the audition and was of-fered the job. That same day, Jennifer, whom the station only considered a marginal employee, was dismissed for theft. Because the station did indeed practice racial discrimination on a regular basis, they didn't even consider firing Finesse for the same infraction. Instead, they offered him a $10,000 bonus if he agreed to totally turn his back on Jennifer, whom they feared would still come after them with a lawsuit.

Since his momma didn't raise no fool, Finesse accepted the job and bonus, and turned his back on Jennifer. As a result, he'd been smiling in front of the cameras ever since.

Destanie was then hired to take Jennifer's place. At first they had a casual and respectful, professional relationship, but after a while, Destanie and Finney became an item. Kind of.

But that was old news. That was then; this was now. Destanie knew the deal when they first hooked up. From jump, he made it clear that he wasn't looking for any attachments; he was just interested in kickin' it. That was the best he could do because he was dating two other women at the time. He told her he was only 28 and not interested in doing the "couples" thing. Finesse knew that her getting attached was not *all* her fault; he shouldn't have thrown it on her like he did.

As he jumped in his car to leave the station, he could still remember the first time he and Destanie were together. They had sex in every position they could think of on a tiny couch in a tiny room at the back of the station. The sex they had that night was so good, they both were immediately whipped. He hated to admit it, but he was getting all hot and bothered just thinking about it.

"What's wrong with you?" he asked himself aloud as his good sense kicked in. "Don't even think about it! She'll never get off your tip; you'll be like Siamese twins—connected at the privates."

"Would that be such a bad thing?" the devil in him asked.

Destanie wasn't so bad when she wasn't being so needy, but Finesse could do without the scenes at work.

As he stopped at a traffic light not far from the station, he mentally relived a few more sexual memories with Destanie. Once he felt the tension in him rise, he got disgusted with himself. *So much for dick control!* "Damn it, Destanie!"

Before he went home, he had a quick stop to make. He made a U-turn in the middle of Broadway and headed toward a familiar neighborhood.

"You are a no-good devil," the sexual scamp in him said aloud.

"No, you're not," his alternate ego responded; "you just like her more than you're willing to let on."

"No you don't," the devil in him countered. "You just want some good lovin', and tonight you should plan on getting exactly what you want."

DESTANIE

Destanie wasn't surprised by the frantic knocking on her front door. She knew Finesse would come to her; they'd been playing the same ritual for about a week. She toyed with the idea of not opening the door, but she couldn't resist him. As long as they both were alive, she planned to always put him first. She wanted to always make him feel special, no matter how it made her feel. Wearing nothing more than a smile, she opened the door and greeted him.

Her body was calling his name! The look on his face was just the reaction she'd hoped for.

"Destanie, I am so—"

"Shhh. You've done too much talking today already. No more." She guided him into her world, a world he desperately wanted and needed to be in.

Like a sinner confronted by Jesus, he followed her commandments obediently once they found their way to her bed, her sanctuary.

Almost immediately, her legs snapped open, enticing him with a whiff of the juices from her frothy wetness. She whispered, "Remember what I've always said—treat me like an angel, and I'll show you heaven."

He kneeled at the altar of her love and did exactly as he was told—*"No talking . . . touch me here . . . kiss me there . . . suck this . . . lick that . . . don't forget the condom."*

As usual, the sex was incredible, but instead of being thankful for allowing him into her temple of worship, Finesse shifted into asshole mode the minute they were done. He slid off the condom, placed it on the dresser and disappeared into her bathroom.

"Look, I don't want you to think that just because you served yourself to me butt naked on a platter that means I'm trying to get back with you. I like you and all, but I'm not looking for anything serious," Finney said from the bathroom.

"Mmmm-hmmm. Goodbye, Finesse."

"Huh?"

"I needed some closure with you, and you just gave it to me," she said calmly.

"B-but I-I thought—"

"What? What did you think, Finney? Did you think that I've been pining away for you these last few weeks since you kicked me to the curb? I know you've just been using me for sex, and until recently, it didn't matter. You've been just a mindless distraction for me as well. Truth is, I was seeing someone the whole time I was seeing you."

"Who? What's his name?"

"Who said it was a he?" she asked, toying with him.

"Oh, so now you're a lesbian?"

"What do you think, Finney? You know what your personal motto should be?—I'm not a kind, caring man; I only play one on TV."

"You're so mature. You can insult me all you want, if it makes your trifling behind feel better."

"I'm not interested in insulting you; I just want to know why you have to be such a jerk about everything."

"I am what I am, and what I am is a jerk who is single and loving every minute of it!"

"Fine. Then take your single, happy, loving-life behind out of here, and don't you ever come back! Just get out! I have to go! I have to get to the bank to make a deposit, so get out!"

"You can go to the ATM anytime. You don't want me to leave. That's what your mouth says now, but your body was saying something else a few minutes ago."

"My body was saying, 'What a skank ho he is!' Now get out!" She threw a glass from her night-stand in the direction of his head.

He bent down just as it grazed his eye. "Have you lost your damn mind? Now I have to wear double my normal amount of makeup tomorrow on TV!" He wiped the blood from the corner of his eye.

Destanie and her doggone temper—that's another reason he had to cut her loose.

"I said, 'Get out!' " Destanie screamed again while reaching for her clock. She didn't have to tell him again.

As he ran from her apartment, pants around his ankles, blood pouring from the cut above his eye, he was reminded that no matter how great the sex was with Destanie, it just wasn't worth all the headaches and pain.

"She is all kinds of crazy and this will be the last time—the very last time—we will ever be together," he told himself.

"... travel is more than the seeing of sights; it is a change that goes on, deep and permanent, in the ideas of living."
~ Miriam Beard

GERALD

"**Y**ou know, taking care of the kitty costs extra," Gerald St. John teased as he finished servicing his richest client—the one that would soon change the course of his life and make all of his professional baseball dreams come true.

"Baby, I'll pay you whatever you want," his client teased back in a Southern accent that oozed desire.

Gotcha!

As Buffy Bates dressed herself, Gerald St. John observed her closely. She had been a client of his for a while. She was white, thin, in her fifties and perfectly coiffed. The dye in her jet-black hair was obvious, and her cat-like facial features suggested that she had been addicted to plastic surgery for some time.

She was actually his first client, and thanks to her and her referrals, Gerald was now the most popular massage therapist at the upscale salon he worked at in southern Kansas City.

Tall and handsome, Gerald St. John was the most popular massage therapist because he was the most liberal with his touch and his tongue. Also, he often sold drugs—mostly coke, meth, and heroin—to the hoity-toity folks who visited the spa on a regular basis. As a drug dealer, he was committed to anyone willing to meet his hefty prices.

He mostly made his living selling mind-altering substances to the rich people who lived in a privileged world that was far different from his own. Gerald made good money when it came to the drugs and "extra services" he offered his clients.

Gerald loved performing oral sex, and needless to say, his enthusiasm resulted in him being booked often months in advance.

The one client he didn't provide "extra services" to was the one client he would've given those services away to for free. Gerald pictured Dr. Madetra Price and smiled. He admired her dedication to the community and her skills as a doctor. So that he could have an excuse to spend time with her, he actually volunteered his massage services to some of her clients at her clinic once a month at no charge.

Watching her in action helping her patients nearly took Gerald's breath away and made him long to spend even more time in her presence. That's why he decided to join her travel club at her invitation. Madetra had intentions of hooking Gerald up with her sister, but he had intentions of his own.

Madetra Price aside, Gerald had plenty of female clients who benefited from his "extra services," and they absolutely loved him; their men loved him too, including Buffy's husband, one of the front-office managers for a semi-pro baseball team. Buffy had been with Gerald since the beginning, and week after week of getting "serviced," he knew she left the spa craving sex. She went home and did her husband every way imaginable; in fact he actually came by the spa once to thank Gerald.

As it turned out, Buffy's husband grew to love spa days just as much as his wife. She once told Gerald that on spa days she could easily count on four orgasms—once during her rubdown, once during her oral therapy, and at least twice later at night with her husband.

Add a little of Gerald's coke and other drugs to the mix, and Buffy was good to go.

For all the pleasure that twenty-seven-year-old Gerald added to Buffy's life, she owed him, and he thought it was finally time for her to put up or get shut down. She knew he desperately wanted to play baseball for one of the local teams. He'd played baseball most of his life, including in high school.

Gerald actually received an offer for a full college scholarship to pitch, but while hanging with some knuckleheads from high school, he got mixed up in the wrong things and wound up spending a little time in jail for robbery and assault.

When Gerald got out of prison a few years later, he wasn't the least bit interested in going to college. He just became bitter and withdrawn and started dealing drugs back in his neighborhood on the northeast side of town.

He'd only recently revived his dreams of playing pro baseball when his P.O. helped him get a job at the spa and he landed Buffy as a client. This was when she came to find out that he desperately wanted to play baseball for one of the local teams.

"So, Buff, what do you say?"

"I say, you're the best," she purred.

"I'm glad you think so, but as you know, I'm not interested in doing this spa thing the rest of my life."

"Why not? You've truly got a God-given talent."

"You know what my real talent is—baseball. I've tried to be patient, but I was just wondering, when do you think you can get me that walk-on tryout?"

"You've met my husband; he's eternally grateful to you. Anytime you want to try out, you can. Just let me know when you're ready, dear boy," Buffy said as she patted his face.

"I'm ready now. I'd like to walk on this week . . . maybe tomorrow if possible—oh, I can't tomorrow; I'm going to that travel club meeting I told you about last week. What about the next day? Can you get me a tryout the day after tomorrow?"

"I think they need a little more time than that, but I'll talk to my husband." Buffy blew him an air kiss and walked out the door.

Gerald knew she was just stalling. Buffy was a lot of things, but a fool wasn't one of them. He knew there was no way she was going to lose her favorite massage therapist to the silly game of baseball. He realized he was going to have to work hard on her—maybe even do some after-hours freaky stuff—in order to get what he wanted. Hell, what was life without a little scandal?

It wouldn't be his first time. Rich white women loved to feel like they were doing something scandalous—and doing a much younger man in their husband's bed topped the list. With Buffy, he was prepared to do whatever he had to do.

MADETRA

"If Oprah can do it with her book club and her Angel Network, so can we," Madetra told her sister the next evening as they prepared the clinic conference room for their first travel club meeting.

"How hard is it really to start a club?" Kaylantra, her identical twin sister, asked.

The travel club really didn't start off as a club. Madetra had made her husband commit to taking more vacation time off work. She made him promise to take her on one fabulous trip every quarter. When she told her twin sister about it, of course she wanted to join them.

Thinking the more, the merrier, Madetra then invited her attractive massage therapist, hoping he'd hit it off with her sister. He, in turn, unfortunately told Dr. Dumb Ass, who was also one of Gerald's massage therapy clients.

From there, Madetra got carried away and invited a local TV producer who had recently produced a wonderful story on the clinic. The producer told her boyfriend—the TV anchor that'd interviewed Madetra at length for the news report about the clinic—and before Madetra knew it, a travel club with seven people was born.

"I can't believe we're going to do this," Madetra squealed. "It should be fun, right?"

"It's going to be off the chain," Kay said, reassuring her with a hug.

By seven o'clock, all of the travel club members had arrived, and after ten minutes of informal chitchat and introductions, the meeting began.

"I think you all know me. I'm Madetra Price, and this is my twin sister Kay, Kaylantra Ellis, and we want to thank everyone for coming out tonight. This is kind of a new thing for me. I don't belong to a lot of organizations, and I'm certainly not normally a person who starts up social groups just for the heck of it. But when faced with the opportunity to do something new and fun, I thought, 'Why not?' This all got started when me and my husband Darryn originally planned on taking a few fun vacations."

Kay chimed in. "I kind of invited myself along, and so did a few others here, and before you knew it, we had ourselves a travel club. Now, as a club, I hope you all are prepared to have a good time! To get this party started, we thought it would be fun if we gave ourselves a name. My sister and I thought of this—*Destination: Anticipation Travel Club.* What do you think? Do you like that? If you don't, we can come up with something else as a group. For short we could call ourselves DAT Club!"

The whole group started laughing. "Okay, DAT Club it is!" Kay announced, energized by the group's enthusiasm.

"I guess the next order of business is to go over the itinerary," Madetra said in an all-business tone. "Since this started out as a personal thing, two of the trips have already been planned, but this group is going to run as a democracy when it comes to the other trips. Whatever the majority wants to do is what we'll do."

Kay spoke up. "This August, in just a few weeks, we're going to go to Minnesota and the Mall of America, and during the month of January, we're going skiing MLK weekend at Lake Tahoe. We have open vacation slots for April and August. Does anybody want to suggest some places we could go?"

"How about Las Vegas in August?" Gerald suggested. "I've never been there before and would love to get my gamble on."

"Sounds good. Any objections?" Mad asked.

Silence filled the room.

"Okay, Vegas in August it is. And now we have one more trip. What would you like to do in April?"

"I have an idea—let's do something really wild," Destanie said, eyeing a bored-looking Finesse. "I mean off the chain, out of the box, buck wild!"

"Okay . . . anybody got any ideas?" Mad asked.

"How about a trip to a nude resort?" E'an suggested.

Everyone in the group fell silent and stared at him, but then one by one, folks started coming around, starting with the men.

"That's a great idea," Finney said. "This travel club is supposed to be all about having fun, right?"

"It sure is," Darryn said.

"Count me in . . . way in," Gerald said with a laugh.

"Ladies, are you okay with that? I personally am not interested in going to a nude beach," Madetra said.

The idea of spending time at a nude resort with E'an, a man that was sexually harassing her, sent chills through her.

"I'm all about getting buck wild!" Kay announced. "And from what I've heard, clothing is optional at most nude beaches; you don't have to walk around in the buff if you don't want to."

"I say we do it!" Destanie said.

"Let's take a vote. Who wants to go to a nude beach as one of our vacations?" Madetra asked.

Madetra sighed when six out of the seven people in the room raised their hands. "Okay, fine, a nude resort it is," she said in a dejected tone. "Does anyone have any ideas on exactly which resort we should go to?"

"I'll do some research and get back with you," E'an volunteered, undressing her with his eyes.

Madetra continued, "I'm going to keep the budget down to one thousand per trip. That includes everything—food, travel and hotel. I'll need you to pay two weeks in advance before every trip, or of course you're all welcome to pay four thousand for all the trips right now. And just in case you're worried about this being legit, if there is ever a problem, you all know where to find me. I'm not going anywhere; my patients wouldn't let me!"

Everyone laughed as they pulled out their check-books and started writing.

"All right, that's it. Any questions? I have all your e-mail addresses, and I'll send you receipts and detailed itineraries tomorrow. Our first trip is in a few weeks! See you then."

"The soul of a journey is liberty, perfect liberty to think, feel, and do just as one pleases."
~ William Hazlitt

E'AN

E'an was a happy man.

The look on Madetra's face the night before during her travel club meeting when he suggested they travel to an *au naturel* beach was priceless—just like the sex he was having with Thalia in Madetra's office.

It was during the lunch hour, and Madetra was gone. Luckily Thalia wasn't a screamer, so instead of getting physical with her after hours when he had much better things to do, he took her whenever he could in Madetra's office.

Talk about priceless.

If Madetra ever saw the two of them climaxing all over her desk and patient records, she'd die on the spot. The very thought made E'an chuckle.

"What's so funny back there?" Thalia asked, between grunts.

"Nothing," E'an responded, the scent of their lust hovering in the air.

He looked at the pictures on Madetra's desk of

her and her husband. Sometimes he wished he could be the man in the pictures with her and at other times, he found the thought absurd. He didn't know how it would happen, but as a result of his membership in her travel club, he had every intention of getting to know Madetra more intimately.

As usual, while thinking of Madetra, he climaxed.

"Wow! That was nice. I should be thanking you," Thalia said as E'an pulled out of her, satisfied.

"Yeah, you should be."

She gave him a dirty look and pushed him away. She then pulled up her undies and adjusted her clothes.

With all the movement, E'an got a whiff of her. "Have you been drinking on the job?" he asked incredulously.

"Uhmmm, yeah—I can have sex on the job but not drink? Be for real."

"*You* be for real. This is a place of business, and professionalism is a must when dealing with patients. You are soooo fired! You have lost your mind."

"No, *you've* lost yours! I can sue you for sexual harassment. Just like I reek of booze, I reek of you. Maybe some of my co-workers might like a whiff."

She grabbed for her purse, missed, and knocked it to the floor.

While she bent down to pick up its contents, E'an noticed that there were several driver's licenses with her picture on them and credit cards—all with different names. Many of them he recognized as clinic patients!

"Tell me I'm not seeing what I'm seeing!" He

pushed her out of the way and snatched up the credit cards and licenses. "Have you been stealing our patients' identification? Madetra was right! Could you be more crazy and ghetto? If this ever got tied back to us and the clinic, we could all lose everything. I will have you arrested for identity theft if you don't get out of here now! And if you tell anyone about what's been going on, especially in this here office, you will never ever get a job in Kansas City that pays more than minimum wage—you got that?"

"You can keep this sorry job!" she yelled. "And you can keep that old, sorry, dried-up witchdoctor of yours too. I hope that uptight thang takes care of you; she has you sprung. You are so out there for her and you don't even know it. She's going to put a hurting on you; just you wait and see. You better watch your back!"

"No, you better watch yours!" He watched her go with a great deal of satisfaction as she ran through the reception area and out the front doors.

Once he was sure Thalia left, he turned on Madetra's computer and started searching the World Wide Web. He had promised her that he'd do research on a nude beach that DAT Club could visit, and this was one research assignment he was looking forward to.

KAYLANTRA

K ay loved Thursdays.
It was her busiest night at the HOTGIRLZ
Strip Club and her best day online at alwayshot
&ready.com. She always heard from SoulViewer
via her site, before she went to the club and that always made her head to the club with a smile on
her face as wide as the ocean.

There was something about the anticipated
weekend that made men weak, and ready to spend
their money and that made Kay smile too.

She'd been dancing at one of Kansas City's most
popular clubs for nearly two years, and Thursdays
during that time had been very lucrative for her.
At HOTGIRLZ alone, she managed to easily pull
in over a thousand dollars a night, and that was
from just one patron. He was someone who'd just
started coming around in the past few weeks.

He would be there soon. After all, it was Thursday. Their day. Whenever he was there, she could
feel him feeling her; she could sense him sensing

her; she could feel his presence from every direction. With every move she made, she felt his hungry eyes on her.

Just knowing he was watching made her want to put on an extra special show just for him. Although she really didn't know who he was—she had never actually seen the face of her secret admirer, not that it really mattered—the less she knew, the better.

For the past month her special patron had requested that she perform $1,000 lap dances for him—blindfolded. At first she bristled at the idea of the bouncers in the club blindfolding her, but then she started to enjoy not being in control. Not having the use of all of her senses helped heighten the senses that she could use. It was all intoxicating and a big turn-on.

For the first two weeks, they followed the club's strict don't-stick-it, don't-lick-it, no-touching policy. But somewhere during that third week, she just had to feel his touch, and from the early days of soft kisses and a little rubbing they had long since been getting their freak on. They were able to flat out have protected sex as long as they kicked back a little to the club. She did lap dances all the time, but he was the only one there that she went all the way with.

He had huge hands and other huge parts that kept her satisfied, but after all this time, she had reached the point where she wanted more. She wanted to see his face, hear his voice, learn his identity.

"Kay, get your fine behind in here! You know what time it is!" Eddie Payton, one of the providers of her livelihood yelled from the breadbox he called an office. "Get in here, girl, now!"

Kay hated that those were often the first words she heard whenever she showed up for work. Like a child about to be punished, she walked slowly into Eddie's office.

"Take off your clothes," he told her without looking up; "you know the drill."

"Don't make me slap you today, Crazy! Do the words sexual harassment mean anything to you?"

"Do the words *never work in this town again* mean anything to you? You've made a lot of people in this town upset with your smart mouth and uppity ways. Your twin sister may be a doctor, but you, my dear, ain't nothing but a working girl, a stripper, a piece of tail."

Defeated and disgusted, Kay stripped naked, slipped a condom on Eddie, and climbed into her overweight lover's lap.

"Dang! You're hot," he said as he spanked her a little too hard.

She had to catch herself and check her temper to keep from knocking him out of his chair.

Actually, being with Eddie wasn't all bad. In addition to tipping her $100 every time they were together, sex with him was like breathing. It took no thought, no effort.

He jiggled her breasts, and she played with his limp member, Mr. Weiner. She then climbed on top of it and wiggled her hips a little, throwing in a bit of moaning as a bonus. In five minutes flat they were done.

"Had you screaming there, didn't I?"

"Yep," Kay lied, "like a hyena."

No longer eager to see her regular Thursday lap dance patron, Kay told Eddie she was going home sick and grabbed her clothes and money and left. She hated herself for always giving in to Eddie but she truly felt like she didn't have a choice.

Her parents had died when she was still a teenager, and while Madetra got scholarships and loans to go to college, Kay got squat. That's when she started dancing.

She had danced in pretty much every club in town, but her smart mouth and temper always got her kicked out and banned. She knew she had no real skills and that the time to take advantage of her looks would be short.

Kay knew she could never work in retail or in an office. She was too money-hungry, and the dough from those jobs would never be good enough. So she took whatever treatment Eddie had to offer.

With any luck, she hoped he'd keel over and die, but until that time she was going to do what she had to do in order to secure her financial future. And if she had to "do" Eddie, then so be it!

"All journeys have secret destinations of which the traveler is unaware."
~ Martin Buber

DARRYN

Darryn Price had always had a strong sexual appetite. In college, he always knew how to keep it fun and exciting, but after eleven years of marriage to Madetra, it seemed as if they had gotten too old for fun and exciting. At least she had. He got the distinct feeling that if she could get away with it, she would be more than happy to never have sex with him again.

He stared at the French maid costume he'd just purchased and started writing a note for his wife.

It was Thursday. She was working late at the clinic—it was massage night—and he was going out for a bit. But when he came home, he wanted to see his wife in that costume and ready to go.

He desperately needed a recharge. He needed to have her tickle his privates. That was the innocent phrase that they had used for sex since college. He needed some good lovin'. He was long overdue. It had been two days.

Many would have considered his screw-everyday sexual appetite unreasonable, but life as an accountant for one of the biggest consulting firms in the city was hard and he needed to release a lot of stress.

He knew Madetra would probably flip when she saw his note and the costume, but he didn't care, *she'd get over it.*

Here lately, the last thing she usually wanted to do was sexual role-play, but Darryn was the opposite—he loved pretending to be something he wasn't.

Over the years, they'd done it all—innocent student/stern principal, firm boss/eager worker, prostitute/pimp, porn star/photographer, frigid woman/sex therapist, stewardess/passenger, stranger/stranger—but it had been a long time since they played the roles of loving husband and wife. At least, that's what his wife always said.

Truth be told, he always thought she wouldn't think twice about killing him. From the very depths of her soul, she wanted him dead. That's how he felt sometimes when he demanded sex. But she knew the Cosmos wasn't having that.

He was the luckiest man on Earth—the Golden Boy, the Chosen One; or so everyone thought. Without much effort on his part, he'd spent a lifetime being lucky. With the intake of every breath, his luck became more and more apparent. All he did was simple.

Breathe—doting parents. *Breathe*—star high-school athlete. *Breathe*—honor student. *Breathe*—college valedictorian. *Breathe*—successful businessman. *Breathe*—married to perfect wife who loved him without question . . . sometimes. *Breathe*—beneficiary to an insurance windfall after his parents' untimely death in a house fire.

Suddenly, Darryn couldn't breathe. He had to remember to breathe. While everyone thought he was perfect, Darryn knew the truth—he was just human, a human whose marriage was slowly coming undone.

Nowadays, whenever he looked at his wife, there was something in her eyes, something unyielding, unforgiving; it let him know that she didn't think he was perfect. Not in the least. Not anymore.

They'd met in college. She was a star on the swim team, and he ran track and was a Kappa Alpha Psi frat boy playa.

They hung out in the same sports circles. They'd dated each other exclusively for two years before getting married. Darryn was the first man to ever leave his imprint on her mind, body, heart, and soul. He changed the way she viewed love.

Prior to him, Madetra hadn't given love much thought at all. She only had one boyfriend in high school, and they'd never slept together. Darryn was the only man she had ever been with, a fact that he was proud of.

From the moment they met, she made it clear that she had grown up in the hood and wanted a better life for herself and her sister. She was determined to be a doctor.

Madetra had graduated from high school by the time she was sixteen. Her parents had died before he met her, during her first year in college. She went to school year-round and received her medical degree in record time. She was by far the youngest student in her graduating class. She basically put herself through school with the help of scholarships and college loans, while her less ambitious sister mooched off of boyfriends, relatives, and friends, and worked at strip clubs.

He shook his head when he thought of Kay. He had always been intrigued by the fact that Madetra and her twin sister were so different in temperament. But then again, Madetra was different from a lot of women. While other girls went to college to *find* doctors that they could marry, Madetra went to college to *be* a doctor—that impressed him.

Darryn opened her world up to new things that she'd never had any interest in, like poetry, jazz, art, and history.

He had serious "whip appeal" from day one and insisted that she bring her A-game to bed every time they had sex. Originally it was something she was glad to do.

For years, she seemed to love sex as much as he did. But lately, ever since he had started going out more frequently, she always complained about being too tired to have sex. She claimed her around-the-clock caring for patients was taking its toll and whined about him always begging her for sex and not spending quality time with her.

Well, he had the perfect plan for spending quality time together tonight—a little bedroom role-playing—and if it didn't work, it wouldn't matter, because going elsewhere was always an option.

DESTANIE

Destanie seethed inwardly as she silently watched Finesse deliver the news.

The first time they slept together about seven months ago, she got pregnant. Neither of them could believe it, because it was such a rookie mistake. Finesse begged her to have an abortion, and she did so, only after he led her to believe in the possibility of a long-term future together.

Well, that blew up in her face. Within six months, Finesse told her that he no longer wanted to see her because things had gotten "too complicated." And with the exception of a recent week-long spat of booty calls, he did all that he could to stay away from her outside of work.

The mistake of having that abortion was finally catching up with her. During her lunch hour, Destanie did her annual visit with her gynecologist and received some terrible news. While she'd always had a problem with fibroids, it never really concerned her. But while doing an ultrasound to monitor the fibroids, her OB/GYN discovered something alarming.

Because of the abortion, Destanie had developed endometriosis, excess scar tissue, and an awful infection. Her condition affected her ovaries and fallopian tubes, and would eventually require surgery, including a full hysterectomy.

It was official—she would never be able to give birth to a child of her own. In her eyes there was only one person to blame—Finesse Brown—but that didn't stop her from loving him and obsessing over him.

Since they had last slept together, Destanie couldn't get him out of her mind. Things had been really icy between them since their last rendezvous, and attending the travel club meeting hadn't helped. Destanie was relying on the travel club to bring them closer together. She was thrilled about the prospect of going on four vacations with him, and while they would be four working vacations with five other people around them at all times, she was optimistic that the time away from the office and in fun environments would be all that it would take for Finesse to realize how much he needed her in his life.

Destanie came to realize a long time ago that what she felt for Finesse was very one-sided but was determined to get him to see her for what *she* felt she was—his backbone, his rib, his strength, his soul mate.

"So how did I do?" Finney asked once his broadcast was over, pulling Destanie out of her wishful state.

"Fine. I-I-I wasn't really paying attention."

Finesse shook his head. "That's not exactly what a news anchor wants to hear from their producer."

Destanie sighed.

"So what's up with you? You've seemed distracted and distant all afternoon."

"What do you care?" she asked with an attitude.

"Don't go getting all upset. I just asked."

"Finney, what would you do if I told you that abortion I had seven months ago made me sterile?"

"What do you mean what would I do?"

"What would you do?"

"What could I do?"

"That's what I thought."

"So, you're sterile? I suppose that's my fault."

"Isn't it?"

"We decided together that it was best if you had that abortion; I didn't make you do anything, so you can't go blaming your inability to have children on me."

"You're such an ass."

"Look, I don't mean to be insensitive, but what am I supposed to do? What can I say? If I had a magic wand that could magically make you fertile, I'd use it in a heartbeat."

That was more compassion than she had expected from him, and it touched her in a way that surprised her. "I'm not blaming you," she said, blinking back tears.

"Good." He reached out and hugged her. "I'm glad."

"I have found out that there ain't no surer way to find out whether you like people or hate them than to travel with them."
~ *Mark Twain*

MADETRA

It was August and hot in Kansas City. Madetra couldn't wait to get away. At first, she wondered if anyone in DAT Club really wanted to go to Bloomington, Minnesota to the Mall of America for their first trip, but surprisingly as they all waited to board the plane, everyone seemed excited.

Not only would there be more shopping than one person could stand at over 520 stores like Bloomingdale's, Macy's, Nordstrom, Ann Klein, and The Gap, but there would also be plenty of time spent visiting the Mall of America's famous centerpiece—The Park at Mall of America, the largest indoor family theme park in the nation.

She herself loved amusement rides and couldn't stop thinking about the spiraling roller coaster and the bright lights of the Ferris wheel that welcomed visitors to MOA. Add to that flight control stimulators, an aquarium, and the chance to see some NASCAR racing, and she knew this was a perfect first trip for DAT Club.

MOA had been around for years, but Madetra had never gotten around to going there to check it out. Considered the largest enclosed retail, dining and entertainment complex in the United States, there was going to be plenty to do.

The plan was to spend the first two days shopping. Day three in Bloomington would be spent at the amusement park and viewing attractions like the aquarium, and then the final two days would be spent driving along the North Shore of Lake Superior, visiting sites like Gooseberry Falls, state parks, famous shipwrecks, and lighthouses associated with Lake Superior, like the Split Rock Lighthouse.

While waiting to board the plane, Madetra, absorbed in her thoughts, didn't notice her husband, who was standing off to the side, looking bored. He tried for several minutes to catch her attention, and when he finally did, he gave her a big, toothy grin. She couldn't help smiling back.

As much as Darryn got on her nerves sometimes, especially when it came to his preoccupation with sex, Madetra still loved him. Darryn was her rock. Smart, handsome, and down-to-earth, he had been such a blessing for her, providing the sturdy foundation she needed. She met him shortly after her parents died in a car accident, and since that time, he and her sister had been Mad's only family.

And while they had never been a fun couple, mostly because he didn't even have a hint of a sense of humor, Darryn did bring a lot of other good qualities to the table.

Madetra looked her husband dead in the eyes and motioned for him to come to her with her index finger.

Darryn walked casually over to her, smiling the whole time. He kissed her square on the mouth once he reached her side, sparking throughout her body a sense of calm that had been missing all morning.

Evil, jealous glances from both E'an Shaw and Gerald St. John were lost on Darryn and Madetra as they talked, laughed, played and otherwise enjoyed each other's company.

"So, how is my baby doing?" Darryn asked.

"I'm a little nervous. I just want everyone to have a good time."

"They will. They'll get what they give. If they're determined to have fun, they will have fun."

Madetra laughed. "Well, the control freak in me wants to make them have fun."

"Do you regret that DAT Club has grown into this monster? Do you wish it was just the two of us like originally planned?"

"It is what it is. The more the merrier, I guess. How about you—do you wish it was just us?"

"Actually, I do," he said quietly as he kissed her again on the lips.

"We will have plenty of time for just us," she said feeling guilty.

"I know. I'm going to enjoy each of those 'just us' moments as much as I can."

"So am I," Madetra said with a smile. "Oh, look, there she is! There's Kay, late as usual." She waved at her sister, who waved back as if she didn't have a care in the world.

"Dang! Kay," Darryn started, "you were supposed to be here over an hour ago. You'll never get your bags checked in time to get them on the plane, and I ain't helping you carry all that crap on board."

Kay gave her younger sister by five minutes a big hug and kissed her on the cheek. Then she told Darryn, "Uhmmm . . . last time I checked, both of my parents were dead, and ain't nobody asked you for your sorry-ass help. Don't make me slap you today, Crazy."

Kay couldn't stand her brother-in-law and couldn't understand what Madetra saw in him. She didn't find him particularly nice, attractive, or well-bred, but according to Madetra, he knew how to throw it on her. So apparently, in Mad's book, that made up for everything else that he lacked.

"So why are you late? Or do I want to know?" Mad asked.

"You don't want to know. Is everyone here? Do you want me to take a head count?" Kay asked.

Darryn grunted as Madetra nodded her head vigorously and winked at her sister. "Everyone is here now."

"Whoa! All that beauty in one family—must be in the jeans," Finesse said as he approached Madetra and Kay.

"How long did it take you to come up with that corny line?" Darryn asked with a chuckle.

"I thought it was kind of clever," Kay said. "Is that j-e-a-n-s or g-e-n-e-s?" she inquired laughing. "Hey, you're the television anchor guy, right? You are . . . ?"

"Finesse, but you can call me Finney. You're Kaylantra, right?"

"Yep. Kay. It's nice seeing you again." She shook his hand.

"Dang! We're in DAT Club together. You can come at me better than that, can't you?" Finesse gave her a warm embrace. "I heard they are about to board the plane. Do you need help with your bags?"

"Yes, please," Kay said as she gave Darryn a funky look.

Finesse grabbed her large suitcase and flung it over his back with ease. The two walked off together, leaving Darryn and Madetra laughing.

"My man is smooth. Too bad your sister is crazy. But then again, I guess game will always recognize game; crazy recognizes crazy. They're probably the perfect match for each other," Darryn observed.

"That was pretty smooth on his part—I have to give it to him—but you were smooth like that once, babe, you know, back in the day."

"Are you trying to say I've lost my touch?"

"You? Lose your touch? Never, baby, never," Madetra said with a laugh as she patted his cheek.

DESTANIE

Destanie could already tell she was going to hate DAT Club, but no matter what she had to do or expose herself to, she was willing to tough it out. Not only because it allowed her off-the-clock access to Finesse, but because it also was a requirement of her job. And if she wanted to maintain her livelihood, she pretty much had to.

How dare Finney flirt with the organizer's sister so openly and right in front of her! She couldn't believe how deep her feelings for him ran, especially since he'd made it clear from day one that he didn't feel the same.

But like most young women desperate for a man, Destanie was determined to show Finney that she was the one for him. She didn't really mind if he went out and tested the waters with other women because, in the end, no matter how many other women he dated or spent time with, he always seemed to manage to come back to her. It was just a matter of time before he realized what he was looking for was right under his nose. As far as she was concerned, Kay was just another example of Finesse testing the waters.

"So you ready for a good time?" E'an asked Destanie, as he appeared in line behind her.

"I guess I'm as ready as I'll ever be. Aren't you the guy that suggested we go to a nude beach on one of our trips?" Destanie laughed.

"I'm impressed you remember."

"I remember you made quite an impression. There were more than a few mouths that dropped that night. That was truly funny. Why such a wild idea? Are you a frequent visitor to nudist colonies?"

"I don't think they call them that anymore." E'an leaned toward her and laughed. "I just wanted to spice things up. That's one thing you'll learn about me—I like to do the unexpected, the unpredictable; it makes life a lot more fun."

"I guess . . . although there's a lot to be said about predictability and stability."

"I ain't trying to get into no philosophical relationship discussions; I'm just here to have a good time. How about you? Why did you join DAT Club?"

"Work. I had to."

"Work?"

"Yeah. I work for Channel 55. I work with Finesse Brown, the guy over there with Kay. We're covering the trips made by DAT Club from a news perspective. You know, more and more strangers are getting together and doing these kind of things . . . travel clubs."

"With you and your boy here, do I need to watch what I say and do?"

"It depends. A good rule of thumb might be,

would you mind if whatever you say or do was broadcast throughout all of Kansas City?"

"Thanks for breaking it down like that. Having your stuff broadcast around town ain't no joke. So the anchor guy you're here with—"

"Who? Finesse?"

"Yeah, Finesse, is he just working Kay as an angle, a source?"

"Who knows what he does?" Destanie asked with an attitude. "Who cares?"

"Oops, I guess I stepped on someone's toes. Do you have a problem with him being over there instead of being over here with you?"

"He's a grown man; he can do what he wants to do. I'm gonna be all about business; if he wants to be all about getting the booty, that's on him."

"Okay, little angry girl."

Destanie started to say something smart but then decided against it. The last thing she needed was to alienate someone in DAT Club.

"Flight 547 to Minneapolis, now completing its final boarding," a dry, monotone voice announced through hidden loudspeakers.

"Forget Finesse. Forget Kay. Come on, let's have some fun," E'an suggested.

"Amen to that!" Destanie said as she followed E'an onto the plane.

* * * * * * *

A few hours later, members of DAT Club found themselves in the lobby of their hotel, the Minneapolis Hyatt. They were awaiting taxis to shuttle them to the Mall of America.

"So what do you think so far?" Destanie asked Finesse as he stared from his oversized chair at Kay, who was on the other side of the lobby talking to her sister.

He rolled his eyes at Destanie and didn't say a word.

"Finney, I'm not trying to hook up with you, if that's what you think. You can hang out with Kay or whoever else you want to hang out with, as long as our work gets done. The mini-camera the station gave us to shoot everything is a good-quality camera. We should really have some fun with this, and we need to work out a plan on what we're gonna do."

"My personal opinion is that we should talk to everyone that is a part of DAT Club. We need to find out why they joined and what kind of traveling they normally do. Then we can, of course, get the group interacting, and you can shoot me on camera having some fun at the attractions. It's not rocket science, Destanie," he said as he stood and walked toward Kay and her sister.

"Fine, if you don't care, neither do I," Destanie yelled after him.

Watching him walk away filled Destanie with sadness. Where was the man who'd shown her so much compassion when she told him only weeks before that she was sterile? Her sadness was multiplied when she called the station a few minutes later to notify them that they had arrived. With every lie she told her news director about all the time she and Finesse were planning to spend together, the dull ache in her heart grew.

* * * * * * *

DAT Club spent the week bonding as they shopped, rode amusement park rides, spent late nights partying and long days hanging out along the shores of Lake Superior—and Destanie got it all on film.

Unfortunately, while she did all that she could to spend as much time as possible with Finney, Destanie's heart sank when she noticed that he seemed just as hell-bent on spending as much time as he could with the captivating Kaylantra Ellis.

"One's destination is never a place, but a new way of seeing things."
~ Henry Miller

MADETRA

A week after returning from Minnesota, Madetra was looking forward to meeting her sister to compare notes about DAT Club's first trip. It was a beautiful summer evening, and they'd agreed to go walking together at Loose Park, a popular hangout for walkers and dog lovers. As she waited for her sister on a bench near the rose garden, Madetra closed her eyes and basked in the warmth of the sun.

"I need to take a picture of this," she heard her sister say as she approached her. "You look so happy, Mad. I haven't seen you look like that in a while."

"I haven't felt like this in a while. You ready to go walking?"

Before Kay could answer, Madetra jumped up and started walking at a nice pace.

As they made their way around the park, they received plenty of whistles and catcalls from men and women who were in the park and driving by.

"So what did you think about our first trip?" Madetra asked.

"It was nice. I had fun, and it seemed like everyone else in DAT Club did too."

"That's what I thought. I noticed Mr. Finesse Brown seemed extremely taken with you."

"He's a harmless flirt. I wouldn't give that man the time of day," Kay said.

"And why not?"

"He's a TV news anchor. Probably every woman in town is after him, including his crazy producer. Did you see the way that Destanie chick was sweating him?"

"Did I? She needs to be shot. That kind of desperation should be reserved for bad television movies," Madetra said with a laugh.

"I thank God that I've never been that desperate over a man. And speaking of being desperate over a man, how are things between you and your honey? You two seemed chummy on the trip. Did it resurrect your marriage like you hoped?"

"Girl, you have no idea. Darryn was so attentive on the trip, and he's been even better since we got home. He's doing those little important things again, you know."

"Just calling to hear your voice, flowers for no reason, romantic dinners . . ."

"Yep, he's doing the whole nine. And the sex . . . off the hook!" Mad squealed.

"So your little plan is working then?"

"It is, with one exception."

"What's that?" Kay asked.

"His name is E'an Shaw."

"What's he got to do with anything?"

"The man has been sexually harassing me for the past two years, and he only joined DAT Club to bug me and harass me after hours. Having him around makes me uncomfortable."

"He's sexually harassing you? Really? You've got to be kidding me. You don't have to take his mess. Kick him out of DAT Club, and sue him for everything he's got."

"I can't. I have to be nice to him. As expensive as it is to practice medicine where I'm at, it would be even worse if I tried to start up a practice somewhere else. I'm hoping he will eventually get tired of coming on to me."

"Well, guess who else is being sexually harassed?"

"You? By who?" Madetra asked.

"Fat and greasy Eddie—who else?"

"What? Why are you putting up with his mess?"

"Because HOTGIRLZ pays good money and no one else in town would let me dance in their club."

"You could get a real job, you know; you have more going for you than just your body. Unfortunately, you just don't realize it."

"Don't start with the lecture—that's why I don't tell you anything about my jobs."

"I wouldn't call what you do for a living jobs."

"That's what SoulViewer says," Kay responded dreamily.

"Excuse me?"

"He's one of my online customers. Over the last few months I've started bonding with him almost to the exclusion of all the other men who want to do online chats with me. I have this image of him as a sensitive, smart introvert who isn't in a relationship and doesn't like picking up women. He's kind, and compassionate, and always encouraging. He's a really nice guy. We really hit it off."

"Is that before or after he watches you pleasure yourself for money?"

"You're such a snob and a prude. I'm gonna keep shaking what our momma gave us until I can't shake it no more," Kay said with a laugh. "We'll see which one of us is living a life of luxury when they retire."

"Speaking of a life of luxury . . . what are you doing tonight?"

"I'm scared to answer that question. Why?"

"This auxiliary board I belong to is having an auction tonight to benefit the Medical Center. They are auctioning off lunch and dinner dates with celebrities here in town. Do you want to go? I heard a rumor that Mr. Finesse Brown from Channel 55 was auctioning off some of his time. I've been meaning to tell you, but forgot."

"What? He never mentioned a word about that to me on our trip."

"He was probably too embarrassed."

"This I have got to see! Count me in," Kay said giggling.

KAYLANTRA

Kaylantra couldn't wait to see Finesse Brown whore himself out for charity.

The 100 Good Men Celebrity Auction and Art Show really drew a crowd. When Kay arrived with Madetra at the Majestic Theater, she was surprised to see dozens of women of all shapes, colors, and sizes, dressed in exquisite gowns, entering the elegant-looking theater.

"I didn't know desperation in the name of charity was so popular," Kay observed with a chuckle as she and Madetra made their way to their seats.

"I don't care how much it costs," an overweight woman in front of them whispered; "I'm going to get me a good man tonight!"

Her unattractive friend responded, "That's the only way you're going to get a good man—you're going to have to pay for him!"

Madetra and Kay looked at each other and laughed as an attractive female emcee in a curve-hugging, black gown made her way to the podium on stage.

The emcee, who called herself Precious Rose, purred seductively into a microphone as Jill Scott's song, "Brotha," began playing. "Okay, ladies, who wants to start the bids on our first fine piece of sumthin' sumthin'?"

As Finesse Brown appeared on stage and strutted down the catwalk, all the women in the room laughed, clapped, whooped, and hollered appreciatively.

"Remember," Precious Rose said, "all bids for a day-long interaction start at a hundred dollars."

"I bid two hundred dollars," someone yelled.

"I bid two-fifty," someone up front countered.

"Look at these raunchy, desperate women. I know you ain't gonna let them take your man home for two hundred and fifty bucks!" Madetra said with a laugh.

"Two hundred and fifty?" Precious Rose commented. "Are you kidding? You're getting him for a steal. Do I hear three hundred? If you're lucky, you may get the news read to you personally, ladies. What woman wouldn't want to spend a day having this 'Chocolate Kiss' at her beck and call?"

"Three hundred!" someone yelled out.

"Oh my goodness! That's Destanie!" Madetra cried out.

"Really?" Kay asked.

"Yep! Four hundred!" Madetra yelled.

"What are you doing?" Kay asked in disbelief.

"Hooking your behind up!"

"Four-fifty!" Destanie yelled.

"Look at that gorgeous man. Kay, how can you possibly stay away from that? Help the poor man

out. You don't want him going home with someone else, do you? Especially not with Desperate
Destanie."

"I could care less who he goes home with," Kay
said defiantly.

"Five hundred!" Madetra screamed.

"Stop that!" Kay told her.

"Five-fifty!" a woman near the front yelled.

"Bid on him, girl!" Madetra said with a laugh.
"These women ain't playing up in here!"

"Do I hear six hundred?" Precious Rose asked.

"Six hundred!" Destanie yelled.

Kay screamed as she jumped out of her seat.
"One thousand dollars!"

Everyone in the audience, including Madetra,
gasped as Finesse bowed in her direction with an
appreciative smile on his face.

"Do I hear eleven hundred dollars? No? Going
once, twice, he's yours!" Precious Rose purred into
the mic.

*   *   *   *   *   *   *

An hour later, as Kay walked through the Art
Gallery observing art objects for sale created by
members of the 100 Good Men organization, Finesse appeared behind her.

"I need to thank you," he said. "You rescued me.
Things were looking pretty bleak for me back
there. Who would have guessed that you thought I
was worth a thousand bucks?"

"Don't flatter yourself—I did it in the name of
charity. Besides, I'm going to like having you indebted to me for a day."

"I love the thought of being indebted to you,
taking care of your every need and desire."

"You couldn't begin to take care of my every need and desire," Kay said as they shared an awkward glance.

"Uhmmm, I need some liquid courage. Would you like for me to get you a drink?"

"Some champagne would be nice," she said before watching him disappear into the crowd.

"You better enjoy him for the brief minute you got him," Destanie said as she slithered out of nowhere and appeared beside Kay.

"What did you just say to me?"

"Finney. Finesse Brown . . . enjoy him while you can."

"Don't be hating on me because you don't know how to keep your man . . . if he ever was your man."

"You so don't deserve him."

"It's just a freaking auctioned-off date. Get over it!"

Finesse returned with two drinks. "Is there a problem, Destanie?"

"Nope! I was just telling Kay what a lucky woman she was to win your services. See you at work!" she said before slinking away.

"Can you say stalker?" Kay took the drink from Finney.

"Forget her! So when are we going to have our date?" Finesse asked as he gently brushed his hand against hers.

"I-uhmmm-uhmmm—"

Sensing the sexual tension between them, Finesse smiled broadly. "Do you think you could give me an answer some time this year, preferably in the form of a complete sentence?"

"What I have in mind for you is not a date." Kay

pulled a pen out of her purse and wrote her address on his hand. "That's where I live. I need my basement cleaned out. Come over tomorrow, Saturday, around eight in the morning. Make sure you're nice and comfy. I suggest sweats, because my basement is a mess," Kay said before walking away with a smile.

"Stop worrying about the potholes in the road and celebrate the journey."
~ Fitzhugh Mullan

GERALD

Gerald was beyond stoked.

His favorite client, Madetra Price, was coming in for a treatment, and he could hardly contain himself. Thanks to Madetra and his benefactor, Buffy Bates, Gerald had a great time in Bloomington at the Mall of America.

When Buffy, his old homegirl from the spa, told him that she tried but couldn't get him a walk-on tryout with the baseball team her husband managed, Gerald was crushed, but Buffy more than made up for it. She whipped out her checkbook and wrote him a check for $20,000 without a moment's hesitation. As she handed him the check, she told him that she would always be there for him, no matter what.

That's what a man liked to hear.

Ever since he was a young man in elementary school, he'd always had sugar mommas throwing money and material possessions his way, but none of them were as rich as Buffy. She helped him raise his game to a whole 'nother level. Because of Buffy, he was able to quickly replenish his bank account to make up for the $4,000 he'd given Madetra Price for travel club expenses.

He was looking forward to life as a DAT Club member. It would give him a chance over the next year to get to know Madetra better. It would help her see him as more than just soft hands that eased away the kinks in her muscles. She would no longer be able to look at him as just somebody that provided a service to her, even though he would have done it for free, if asked.

Sadly, she was one of the few that didn't let him pet, eat, stroke, nibble, or do anything else to the kitty. That didn't change the fact that seeing her naked on a table and stroking her at the spa once a month was one of his greatest joys in life. But if he could really spend time with her, talking to her, getting to know her, and stroking her mind, he imagined that to be an even greater thrill.

Unfortunately, they didn't get to spend much time together in Minnesota on DAT Club's first trip. But that was to be expected. She was a married woman who seemed interested in spending time with her husband. Plus, she was the group's organizer and she had to make sure her time was divided evenly among everyone that was a part of the group. Despite not spending much quality time with her, Gerald did feel that he got to know her a little better on the trip, by simply observing her and her husband.

Thinking about Madetra's husband tied Gerald's stomach up in knots. While Gerald hated to admit it, he was jealous as hell. Darryn Price was all wrong for Madetra. He seemed like a bit of a loner, and the only times he ever seemed like he was even with Madetra was during those times when she initiated the hand-holding, the affectionate touching, and the passionate kisses.

Another thing Gerald observed was that Darryn didn't seem to show her a lick of respect, at least not the kind she deserved. He seemed to be almost jealous of her and the attention she was getting from everyone else, especially the male members of DAT Club. It was obvious that her husband didn't deserve her, and Gerald was willing to do anything and everything to show Madetra how unworthy her husband was.

For starters, from just looking at him, Gerald could tell he was doing drugs—dealers could recognize addicts easily. From what Gerald could tell, Darryn was in the early stages of his addiction, but addicted all the same, and whatever he could do to help move that addiction along, Gerald intended on doing it.

Gerald also observed E'an Shaw and thought something about him seemed awfully shady. Especially when he saw how E'an acted and treated Madetra on spa night at the clinic. It was obvious to Gerald that E'an had a crush on Madetra, and the thought of another man wanting his precious Madetra made his blood pressure rise. It was clear to him that Madetra had no feelings for E'an and that her feelings for her husband seemed strong.

Not usually being one to put asunder what God had joined together, Gerald was determined to get Doctor Madetra Price, and if she ever came to him expressing interest in being more than friends, he was going to make sure he was available and there for her.

He turned up the soothing music in his massage room and meditated until Madetra's arrival.

"You know you're late, right?" he asked when Madetra walked in twenty minutes later. "Me and my poor behind follows you like a love-sick puppy all the way to Minnesota, and all of a sudden you don't know how to be on time."

Madetra winked at him.

"You can charge me a late fee."

"If I could, I would treat you for free," Gerald said as he winked back.

Madetra didn't know what to say in response to his gentle flirting, so she slipped into the bathroom, took off her clothes, and donned one of the spa's signature fluffy, white robes.

When she returned to the room, Gerald turned his back to her as she slid onto his table, underneath a cottony-soft white sheet.

Once she was settled comfortably on the table on her stomach, Madetra cleared her throat. Gerald turned to face her. He loved their ritual and often wondered if she knew he could see her naked reflection in the window.

"So are there any special problem areas you want me to focus on?"

"My whole body is a problem area," she said with a nervous laugh. "Okay, I can't wait to hear your thoughts."

"About?"

"About DAT Club and our first trip."

"I had a blast. Everyone seemed cool; no one seemed like they were going to bring a lot of drama to the group. It was chill. Nice."

Madetra smiled. "That's what I thought too."

Even though she was a doctor, in so many ways

Gerald thought Madetra seemed young. When he actually reflected on it, he realized she *was* young; in fact, just a few years older than he was.

She reached into her pocketbook and pulled out a picture. She handed it to Gerald. "Check this out—you don't know nothin' 'bout that, kid—that is the next generation of wireless, platinum-plated digital audio equipment. That's what I ordered the other day for my husband."

"That is nice. I could never afford anything like that. It would be odd having a ten-thousand-dollar stereo system up in my two-dollar house."

"I thought it was a three-dollar house," Madetra teased as he kneaded her back.

"Ah yeah . . . appreciation," Gerald said with a laugh.

As he continued to work her over, Madetra let out a deep sigh. She had been coming to the spa for two years, and Gerald St. John had only been her massage therapist for the past six months.

When her female therapist left to start her own spa out of town, Madetra almost cancelled her membership. She had loved her therapist, Sharon, and only decided to stay at the spa when someone told her that Gerald's technique was similar to her former therapist's.

With time Madetra found out this was true. She also found out some other stuff about Gerald . . . some not so great stuff. She knew from other patrons that he not only acted as a gigolo—sexing much of the spa's clientele for money on the side—but he also supplied drugs to anybody and everybody at the spa who wanted them. Despite his less than scrupulous and law-abiding ways, Madetra found his ass intriguing as hell. He was sexy, hot, kind, and if she wasn't married, she was sure that she'd be taking advantage of his other services. She laughed a little too loud at the thought.

"What's so funny?" Gerald asked.

"Nothin'. You just hit my funny bone," Madetra lied, embarrassed by her thoughts. Yep, if she were single, she and Gerald would be having a whole different kind of spa experience, Madetra thought as she closed her eyes and gave into the hypnotic healing powers of Gerald St. John's hands.

MADETRA

Madetra was thrilled with how things were going with DAT Club. Not only were the trip destinations wonderful, but everyone was getting along, including her and her husband, Darryn. Their first trip to the Mall of America allowed them to spend some quality time together, and the sex, without the pressures of everyday life, was wonderful. She was hoping that things would be just as fantastic for them at Lake Tahoe.

As she looked out the window of her suite at the Alpine Mountains she would be skiing on all day, she sighed blissfully. Lake Tahoe was just as she imagined. There were 91 trails at the Heavenly Mountain Resort at Lake Tahoe. Considered a recreational haven, it was known for its world-class skiing and sledding, tubing, mountain biking, hiking, horseback riding, fishing, parasailing, and golf. It had been used as a backdrop location for movies like *The Godfather, Part II; Die Hard 2: Die Harder; Cobb; and City of Angels* and nearby Fallen

Leaf Lake had served as a setting for Whitney Houston's *The Bodyguard*.

DAT Club rented a 6-bedroom town home off the lake, where Madetra and her husband shared a room, and everyone else had their own. Located on 19 acres of pristine wooded grounds, the popular resort they were staying at sat on Lake Tahoe's southern shore. There was a quietness and serenity about the place that Madetra had never experienced, a serenity that she wanted to hold on to and enjoy for as long as she could.

When they'd first arrived the evening before, the group explored the resort and found a quarter mile of private sandy beach that included a pier, outdoor pools, hot tubs, a sauna, and tennis courts. There was also a shuttle service to get them to nearby casinos and other sites in town.

It was Martin Luther King weekend. That meant the winter carnival was taking place, and several black ski clubs were in town. Black folks from all over the country were getting their ski on, partying, and otherwise having a good time.

"Beautiful view, ain't it, baby?" her husband asked sleepily from the other side of the bed.

She pulled the covers off of him, exposing his naked body. "Yes, it sure is."

Darryn laughed. "I was talking about the mountains, silly."

They'd been up extremely late the night before, but instead of being exhausted, they both were surprisingly feeling restless and horny.

"What would you say if I told you I wanted us to get naked and tickle our privates?"

"I'd say, let's get it on . . ." she sang in awful Marvin Gaye fashion. Madetra loved it when he used that "tickle our privates" line. He'd used it on her back in college when she was a virgin and it made an act that she was so afraid of seem so sweet, harmless, and innocent.

At first, with Darryn, things *were* sweet and innocent, but over the years, to keep things spicy in the bedroom, they'd gotten freakier and freakier. From freaky costumes to sexy role-playing to their crazy toys, things sometimes got pretty wild. Not that Madetra minded, because she loved her sex-crazed husband.

But shortly before she started the travel club, things had changed. They weren't getting along well.

Darryn, as usual, wanted sex all the time, not understanding that she not only had to work but also take care of home, which, quite frankly, just wore her behind out. It didn't help that he wanted nookie without offering up a little romance. He no longer did any of the little things that made relationships special, and since she wasn't getting from him emotionally what she needed outside of the bedroom, Madetra found it hard to give him what he needed in bed.

In addition, he'd recently started going out much more frequently. On his nights out, he came home distant, different, to the point where sometimes they almost felt estranged. Their planned vacations together were supposed to change that. She was hoping that time away from the stress of everyday life would allow them to reconnect emotionally and sexually.

"Come on, let's tickle our privates in the shower?" she asked.

"What is it with you . . . sex and water? I'll race ya!"

The two hopped out of bed and ran to the bath-room. Madetra turned on the shower, climbed into the large stall, and let the warm water cascade over her body. Darryn soon joined her. She immediately reached for their vanilla-scented soap and started lathering his body, spending ample time paying special attention to his ever-hardening penis. He returned the favor by lathering her up too.

She gasped when he stuck two fingers inside of her—making sure to cleanse her every crevice—inside and out. Soon afterward, she felt him grab her hips from behind on both sides as he eased his thickness into her hot love pot. She felt every inch of him explore her. She spread her legs, grabbed the railing above the door of the shower, and pushed backward, wedging his hardness deeper inside her. She continued to push back as hard as she could, meeting his every thrust with all that was in her. She felt the heat from between her legs grow, and they became one, as his hand massaged her wet slit.

To him, she felt like silky-smooth satin.

She pushed back on him some more and pumped him harder, faster. She then moved in slow circles so that his member was swirling inside her like a big, thick, stick stirring a rich, velvety cream. "Ahh-hhh," she moaned. "Ahhhh . . . yeahhhhh, baby . . . yeahhhhh!"

They both found themselves panting and grunt-ing from exhaustion. It was pure straight sex at its finest. Together they stiffened and then melted, coming in waves. Both of their bodies thrashed and convulsed as if an electrical shock was radiat-ing through them, one spirit to the other.

She was his conduit; he was hers.

She clamped her vaginal walls tight around his member for a while as the last fluid remains of their time spent together inched down their legs only to be washed down the drain in the shower.

And that was just the first time. Three orgasms later, she was dry, he was spent, and they were both happy. When they were finally done, they untangled their limbs.

Madetra lingered in the path of the water's cleansing stream for a few more moments before stepping out of the shower to dry off. She had forgotten her deodorant and searched for Darryn's in his travel bag. She found more than toiletries. She found a bag of what looked like weed and a dozen blue pills.

At first she wasn't too worried because she knew her husband smoked some occasional weed, but the blue pills were new.

Was it Ecstasy? Something else?

She fought the urge to go question him because they were having such a good time. Madetra decided to wait and confront her husband about what she found once they returned home.

The "just say no to drugs" talk could wait, she thought with trepidation as they prepared for a day of skiing.

"Life is either a daring adventure or nothing. To keep our faces toward change and behave like free spirits in the presence of fate is strength undefeatable."
~ Helen Keller

KAYLANTRA

In Kay's opinion, it had been a great day on the slopes—if she didn't count Destanie following everyone around with a camera, asking annoying questions. But if everything went as she'd hoped, Kay imagined the night would be even better. She and the rest of DAT Club were looking forward to having a good time unwinding at the resort. They had received invitations from five different ski club members to join them for an evening of fun and games.

DAT Club met promptly at six o'clock in the lobby, ready for the fun to begin.

One of the skiing organizers started the evening by welcoming everyone. "I've seen a lot of you stumbling all over the slopes today," she said as the group laughed. "I ain't calling out no names, even though I should. So tonight I thought we could make it a little easy on ourselves and try something not too taxing. Who is up for a game of *Black-*

tionary? We'll be playing in the rec room in ten minutes," she said before disappearing into the crowd.

"What's Blacktionary?" Madetra asked her sister.

Kay shrugged her shoulders. "Who knows? Who cares? More importantly, where is the liquor? And where is your irritating husband? I need to make sure I avoid him."

"I don't know the answer to either of those questions. Now, whatever you do, don't embarrass me tonight. I don't want you thinking you're up in a strip joint. And I sure better not see you shaking your behind on no tables or using the pillars in here as dancing poles," Madetra teased with a broad smile.

"Forget you. I'm going to go find some liquor and indulge in another of my many vices—fine, rich, black men," Kay responded before slinking off into the crowd to begin her prowl.

"So where is your sister?" Finesse asked Madetra a few minutes later.

"She's off looking for liquor and men. So what's up with this game? What's *Blacktionary*? You ever played it before?"

"Yeah, I've played it before—it's black folks' *Pictionary*. Kind of like 'ghetto charades,' but you have to draw the clues instead of acting them out. Do you and the rest of the DAT Club members want to play?"

"I know I do."

"What about your sister?"

"She loves games. Let's see if we can find her and the rest of DAT Club."

They walked slowly to the rec room and felt a little silly because already waiting for them was the whole travel club, along with 13 other *Blacktionary* players.

"Okay, let's make this simple," said the game's organizer. "It's going to be the men against the women. Who wants to be the team captain for each team? The captain will be the one doing the drawing, so if you know you can't draw to save your life, you may want to sit this out," she said laughing.

Finesse and Kay both raised their hands to be team captains.

"Okay, you two come on up and lead the teams. I need you men on one side of the room and you women on the other."

The group did as they were told. While they rearranged themselves, the game's organizer pulled an easel and large drawing pad out of a nearby closet and grabbed some Magic Markers from a nearby desk. People not interested in playing moved toward the perimeter of the room to observe. There were 9 members on each team, plus the captains, and another twenty or so people stood around watching.

Kay pulled a card from the top of the card deck. She then turned toward her team's side of the room and announced, "The category is sitcoms of the '70s and '80s featuring African-American characters." She showed the card to Finney and then sat it down on the table. "Ladies first, right?" she asked.

When the organizer nodded yes, Kay immediately drew a picture of dynamite. Then she drew a cross with a black Jesus on it.

Desperate, Destanie, one of the female team members, jumped up and yelled out a universally recognized classic black sitcom line. "Damn, damn, damn!"

"If you love 'em, we got 'em," the group sang. "Good Tiiiiiimes!"

"Show-offs!" Finney teased as the females in Kay's group high-fived each other.

"Okay, team, it's our turn," Finesse announced. "Let's show those lightweights up."

He looked at the discarded card again. He drew clouds and a high rise with an upward arrow.

"Well, we're movin' on up," one of the men in the group began singing.

Finney pointed at his team and shook his head vigorously.

"WWEEEEZZZZEEEE!" someone screamed out as the crowd laughed.

"The Jeffersons!" Finney's team yelled in unison.

Kay looked at the men and laughed. "Okay, ladies, let's do this! I just know we are going to make those hardheads look bad, right?"

"Hell, yeah!" the women screamed.

Kay looked at the playing card and drew two stick figures, one of a man with a beard, holding his hand over his heart, the other of a younger man, looking at him with a frown. She then drew a trashcan with junk in it and all around it.

"Too easy—Sanford and Son!" Destanie yelled out.

The room erupted into laughter as people sang and danced to the popular show's instrumental theme song. Soon the dancing morphed into an impromptu step show by the men in the room who either in the past or currently belonged to fraternities. As the fraternity men in the room did a unique and sexy step show, complete with throwing up frat signs representing the Kappas, Sigmas, Alphas, and Q Dogs, the women in the room watched from the sidelines, impressed.

"There is way too much sexiness in this one room for me," Kay whispered to Madetra, not realizing that the sexiest thing in the room was standing on the other side of it with his eyes glued on her.

* * * * * * *

Since that night at the auction, Kay couldn't get her mind off Finesse Brown. And ever since they arrived the night before at Lake Tahoe, it was like they couldn't leave each other's sides.

Even when they were skiing or snowboarding earlier during the day, he always managed to get on the lift with her or ride the same hills at the same time as she did. And no matter where they went, Destanie wasn't far behind, although Kay tried to ignore her.

Watching him play "ghetto charades" really turned her on. He was such a breath of fresh air, such a handsome and smart man in a sea of cookie-cutter men, who all acted, talked, and looked the same.

"So are you having fun?" Finney asked while Kay surveyed the buffet table.

"Yep, I am. Are you?"

"The *Blacktionary* thing was scary, huh? Folks in here know a little bit too much about black sitcoms."

"We all need a hobby, huh?"

"Desperately. Might I suggest sex? I know it's my favorite pastime," Finesse said with a flirtatious smile.

"So is sex all you think about?" Kay asked.

"Pretty much. Is that wrong?"

"Depends on who you're thinking about it with," she said with a wink. "For the record, it's my favorite pastime too."

"See, there's something we have in common."

"I guess so," she said, concentrating again on the food and garnishes spread out lavishly in front of them amid Afro-centric decorations.

"I can't make up my mind; I don't know what I want."

"I'll help you," Finney told her. "Close your eyes."

"Excuse me?"

"I'm not going to bite you . . . promise."

"Kill a woman's dream, why don't you?" she said laughing.

When Kay closed her eyes, he placed a piece of barbeque chicken under her nose.

"So, what do you smell?" Finney asked.

"Barbeque chicken, smothered in K.C. Masterpiece sauce with a touch of added lemon." Kay parted her lips and took a bite of the chicken, trying her best to look sexy.

"Man, you're good."

"Lucky guess. What's next?"

"Try this." He took a bite-sized slither of Mozzarella cheese into his mouth, and leaned forward and kissed her, transferring the cheese from his mouth to hers. "What do you think of that?"

She opened her eyes. "I think you better not ever do that again," she said sternly.

"Oh, I'm sorry. I didn't mean to—"

"Let me finish—at least not in public." She smiled and then left.

Always leave them wanting more.

Before she died, that was a lesson Kay's mother had drummed into her head, and she had internalized it, which was evident, from her success at HOTGIRLZ and online.

Given his position, she expected Finesse to be conceited and arrogant, but he wasn't. Yet, she knew in her heart she would never let things go any farther between them. Never! They'd had fun cleaning up her basement together months ago, and now there was this kiss.

She knew she had to stop things before they got out of hand. Being in a relationship with a local television celebrity would draw all kinds of attention to Kay that she just didn't want. Plus, Finesse obviously had a stalker-in-training on his ass! Destanie had proven she was that and more with her clandestine stalking on the slopes and her aggressive attitude the night of the auction.

But those wouldn't be the only drawbacks she'd face if she allowed herself to fall for Finesse Brown. In the past, whenever she'd tried to date men seriously, they always tried to force her to give up her career in the sex industry. She knew eventually she would give up that life, but the time was never right because the money was too good.

As far as she was concerned, Finesse Brown's Mozzarella-flavored kiss was going to be the first and last kiss Kay ever received from him. It was going to be a one-time thing, a one-time thing that she would never forget.

GERALD

Gerald St. John was like most men. In his mind, a sport didn't exist that he couldn't tackle and master. Gerald had never been on a pair of skis before in his life, but that didn't keep him from skipping the easier runs like Patsy's, Groove, Mombo Meadows, Poma Trail, off the Boulder Chair, or Edgewood Bowl, not to mention the ski class for beginners. Instead, he joined the rest of DAT Club on a more challenging run during the group's second full day at Tahoe.

From listening to people talk, he'd picked up two valuable pieces of skiing advice. He learned about the classic snowplow move that involved pointing his skis together to slow down and shifting his weight to turn. Plus, he learned that it was important to ski across the mountain, not down the mountain.

Unfortunately, none of that advice made a lick of difference when he took off wrong, went airborne, and tumbled halfway down a run behind the rest of his travel club crew. With snow jammed into all of his facial cavities, the breath knocked out of him, his ribs aching, and his confidence splintered, Gerald couldn't have felt more foolish when Madetra came back up the hill looking for him. She immediately recognized the seriousness of his situation and demanded that he lay still until a stretcher and medical team arrived.

When the two of them returned to the main lodge an hour later, Gerald's pride, not to mention his entire body, was sorely bruised.

Madetra watched him settle uncomfortably onto an overstuffed couch. "I knew you weren't ready for those slopes. You should have taken a class first."

"I know. I wasn't thinking. So do you think I'll live?"

"Yep. Nothing is broken. You just had the wind knocked out of you, but you're lucky; you could have been seriously hurt."

"No, I'm lucky because I have a great friend like you looking out for me. So are you heading back to the slopes?"

"Nope, I'm staying here with you, that is, if you don't mind. I just want to make sure you're okay. I can't have you suing me or DAT Club for liability and damages."

"The thought never crossed my mind," he said with a smile. "I don't really want you in here babysitting me, though. You need to be out there having fun with your man and the rest of the crew."

"They probably don't even know I'm not out there, and to be honest, I'm not in the mood for skiing. I'm still sore from yesterday. You better be glad you weren't out there then. Where were you, by the way? I hardly saw you or my husband at all yesterday."

"I was just hanging out."

"Well, good. Then you're used to it, because that's all you're going to be doing for the rest of the trip—hanging out right here on this couch."

Gerald winced.

"Are you in pain?"

"Just at the thought of not being able to spend time on the slopes with you."

"Okay, Mister Flirtatious, cut the BS," Madetra said with a nervous laugh.

They spent the rest of the afternoon laughing, talking and enjoying each other's company. He talked about his old dream of playing baseball, and his new one of one day owning his own spa. She talked about her desire to have one of the largest medical practices in the inner city and her desire to one day offer scholarships to young black girls interested in medicine. They hardly seemed to notice when the rest of the group sans Darryn appeared hours later around dinner time.

After dinner, the whole group hung out in front of the fireplace, where they danced and played cards and dominos. And when the women in the group fawned all over Gerald, Madetra was surprised by the feelings of jealousy she experienced.

"I'm going to head to my room," Madetra said around midnight, in a more relaxed tone than she felt. "If any of you see my honey, please let him know that I've turned in for the evening. Good night, all," she said wistfully to the members of DAT Club as they barely looked up from their rousing good time.

"The open road is a beckoning, a strangeness,
a place where a man can lose himself."
~ William Least Heat Moon (William Trogdon)

E'AN

E'an ran up behind Madetra as she was leaving. "Mind if I tuck you in?"

Madetra rolled her eyes. "Are you ever going to stop?"

"It's not likely. So where is your husband? He kind of disappeared while we were out on the slopes."

"I wouldn't know what happened to him," she answered in a clipped tone. "I had to come back to the lodge and see about a patient."

" 'A patient'—that's what you're calling him?"

"I'm not even going to justify that question with an answer."

"Madetra, tell me something—how is it that you and I got off on such a bad note? If I was an outsider looking in on our relationship, I would think that you hated me."

"And you would be right. Call me crazy, but I think our problems may have started when you began sexually harassing me on the first day I started my practice there at the clinic."

"Is that what you think of my innocent flirting? Sexual harassment?"

"E'an . . . you don't do coy well."

"Okay, fine. Let me cut the bull. The truth is, I want you and I want you bad; I've wanted you since the day I first laid eyes on you, and I usually get what I want—you need to remember that."

"You are pathetic!"

"I *really* wanted you today when we were all in the gondola riding over to the top of the mountain."

"What?"

"I've always wanted to have sex high up in the air. Imagine a quickie on a gondola. In twelve minutes, we could give that song, 'she'll be comin' 'round the mountain when she comes' new meaning. Can't you just imagine how positively erotic that would be? The mind-numbing, swaying movement . . . the idea of being inside you . . . gently rocking deep inside of you . . . feeling your excitement and the heat and warmth of your body grow and grow and grow . . . until we both explode together."

"I'd like for you to explode all right."

"Just the thought turned me on earlier today when I looked at you so prim and proper sitting across from me in that tight-ass snowsuit of yours when the group rode over to the mountain together on the gondola. You wouldn't believe how turned on I was by just thinking about being inside of you. I'm surprised you didn't notice my woodie right then and there."

The minute E'an finished his sentence, Madetra slapped him. "I've swallowed my pride and taken a lot of mess off of you because I've been afraid of losing my practice, but don't you ever in your life, as long as you are black, talk to me that disrespectfully again or I will sue the hell out of you! Do you understand me?"

"Sue me? With what evidence? It's always only you and me when we have our little conversations. He said versus she said. I've never put anything in writing. I never have, and I never will."

"You never know, E'an, I may one day soon invest in some high-tech recording equipment. I may have it on me at all times, and who knows what I might pick up?"

"It wouldn't be admissible in court," he told her smugly.

"Wanna bet your livelihood on that?" Madetra asked before she turned on her heels and walked away.

DESTANIE

"Listen to what just the thought of you does to me, Finney . . . ahhhhh . . . yeahhh . . . yes . . . yes . . . yes!" Destanie screamed before climaxing into the phone.

While they were dating, Destanie left cum messages like that for Finesse every morning whenever they didn't spend the night together. Although they were no longer together, she continued to leave cum messages for Finesse on his cell phone after returning from Lake Tahoe.

She knew it was downright crazy to leave him those messages now. Heck, a whole new level of vocabulary beyond "crazy" was needed to describe her actions; but Destanie didn't care. She wanted to make sure Finesse knew just how much she was thinking of him and just how much she wanted him. Not only did she leave dirty messages, but she also constantly sent him naked pictures of herself and sent him sexually explicit poems and e-mails.

Destanie hadn't always been so open with her

sexuality. Finesse brought out the inner freak in her that for years had been lying dormant. Before him, when it came to men, she didn't have that much experience, but despite that, she'd developed a pattern.

She'd only been with four men in her life, including Finesse. Their names and faces were now indistinguishable. Their love, which once seemed so important, now meant less than nothing, but there was a definite pattern with her relationships.

Girl meets boy. Girl likes boy. Girl and boy get together. Girl and boy hook up and have sex. Girl gets on boy's nerves. Boy breaks up with girl. Girl wants to have boy killed. Girl gets a grip that is unfortunately only temporary. Girl wants boy to fall off the face of the earth. Girl has change of heart and loses all self-restraint in an ill-fated attempt to win boy back by stalking him.

It wasn't a pattern Destanie was particularly proud of, yet it was a pattern she couldn't seem to change. For simplicity sake, Destanie nicknamed her boyfriends "Restraints 1–4," when she periodically thought of them.

Restraint #1, "The Quicker Picker Upper," was the seemingly normal one. He was a nice, sweet, kind guy who was always trying to clean up other people's messes, including hers. He was the type who always tried to smooth things over and do for others, often at the expense of his own well-being. He was too doggone nice, and everyone knew it but him. He was a Doormat—with a capital D—and she got bored with his tired behind when she'd run out of challenging ways to use him. Ironically, he broke it off with her, because she didn't use him enough, or in his words, "need him enough." She started stalking him when she finally came to appreciate how good a man he really was. The stalking finally stopped when during a particularly ugly stalking episode, he died too young in front of her very eyes from a heart attack brought on by her sudden, unexpected appearance.

Restraint #2, "The Christian," didn't start out that way. A month after their first date, they had sex. It was amazing. It was the kind of sex you had to just thank God for, and speaking of God, Restraint #2 became a born-again Christian approximately six months, three weeks, and two days after they started dating. They broke up two days and 12 hours after that.

Once he was saved, he wouldn't touch her with a ten-foot pole. He told her he wanted to save himself for marriage and that he didn't see that marriage occurring with her. She stalked him for a year after that and only stopped when he changed his name, became a preacher and moved to the other side of the country.

Restraint #3, "The Thug," was the scariest of the bunch. He had a big mouth and violent temper. He'd been shot three times by three different people and would get into a fight at the drop of a hat. If you looked at him funny, accidentally bumped into him, or showed him any other type of perceived disrespect, you'd best be prepared to throw down and defend your honor. But Restraint #3 wasn't all bad; he did have some redeeming qualities. He was loyal to a fault. For the people he truly cared about, he'd lay down his life. He'd fight alongside you to the death. He'd loan you his last dollar, give you the shirt off of his back, and then beat you down if you didn't return it in a timely manner. She didn't stalk him long because he eventually threatened to turn his violent temper against her.

And finally, there was Restraint-to-be #4, otherwise known as Finesse or "The One." He was the one Destanie planned on spending her life with, despite his obvious growing feelings for Kaylantra Ellis. Finesse was, to put it simply, a cheating, no-good dog. If you looked up the word *dog* in the dictionary, you'd see his picture, but despite his faults, Destanie loved him. She needed him in her life like she needed air.

During the time they were together, he cheated on her with at least two women that she knew about, but at least he was honest about it. He never claimed to love her, nor did he make any outright promises to be with her forever. Yet, the six months she spent loving him were the happiest six months of her life, and she was going to do whatever she had to do—cum messages, dirty photos and all—to win him back.

"The real voyage of discovery consists not in seeing new landscapes, but in having new eyes."
~ *Marcel Proust*

DARRYN

Darryn, Madetra, and the other DAT Club members had been back from Lake Tahoe for just a few days, but during that time, Darryn couldn't fight a growing suspicion that something was wrong with his wife.

Ever since they got back from their first DAT Club trip, things had been really good between them. He was trying to be more attentive, and his wife had been sexing him like she used to—tickling his privates daily with a big old grin on her face. Yet, he could feel something was brewing; he knew it as sure as he knew his own name. Madetra was good at hiding her true feelings and would sometimes wait for weeks to reveal something that was bothering her.

His ass-toe was tingling like crazy. Darryn had a feeling it wouldn't take her that long to come clean, but when she did, he hoped he'd be ready.

Since he'd started going out more, he'd also started drinking more heavily and doing more weed than he was used to. But as far as he knew, his little wife didn't know about his increase in dead brain cells due to his use of mind-altering substances.

"Baby, you up?" Madetra asked as she slid into bed naked beside him. She'd just finished showering after another night of mind-blowing sex, when her scent of vanilla and cocoa butter washed over him.

Darryn was horny all over again, but he didn't dare move. He could sense that tonight would be the night when his wife would finally reveal what was bothering her.

"Honey, you woke?" she asked again.

"I am now," he responded, his curiosity getting the better of him.

"Darryn, there is something I've been meaning to talk to you about, baby," Madetra said in a sweet and innocent tone.

"Talk away."

"When we were at Lake Tahoe, I found some weed and some blue pills in your travel bag, and I was just wondering what was up with that. Also, I noticed you just kind of disappeared on us a couple of times, and I was just wondering why."

"Honey, you know when I'm stressed, I smoke a little blunt, and things have been crazy at the office," Darryn lied.

"That's what I thought, but there was an incredible amount of weed in your bag, baby, more than I've ever known you to have on you. And what about the pills?"

Her sweet and innocent tone started to piss him off. Who the hell did she think she was? He was the authority and head of their household, the master of their domain. He didn't have to explain anything to anyone. He was the king of their castle, and she needed to treat him as such. He ruled their home, not her.

"Those blue pills and how much weed I carry on me are my business, not yours."

Madetra took a deep breath and sat up. Darryn was the epitome of a strong-willed, angry black man, and she knew she had to tread lightly with him if things were to stay civilized and on course.

She hated arguing and wanted to avoid an argument with him at all costs, but she needed some answers.

"Baby, it's just that I'm concerned. You shouldn't be doing speed or Ecstasy, which is what I'm assuming those pills were. I'm bringing this up because I—"

Before she could finish, Madetra felt a stinging sensation spread across the right side of her face as she lay on her stomach several feet from their bed.

"I can't believe you just hit me!" Madetra screamed as she struggled to get up. But her attempts to rise were futile because before she could utter another word, she was laying face down, sprawled out on the floor spread-eagled, with her 200-pound husband's knee in her back.

Her screams were stifled by his hand, which was planted firmly across her mouth. "Shut the hell up!" Darryn ordered.

For good measure, he twisted her arm hard behind her back, and Madetra screamed out in pain.

"I said, shut up! You had to go and ruin everything with your stupid questions. We got along so good on the first trip in Minnesota and at Lake Tahoe. Things are like they were back in our early days. You remember those days, don't you? Back when we were first married eleven years ago . . . when you didn't act better than me just because you were a doctor!"

"Darryn, I don't think I'm better than you, sweetie! Is this what your increased drug use is about?"

"I said shut up with the questions!" he screamed, this time his voice tinged with vulnerability.

"Baby, whatever it is that you're dealing with, we can deal with it together. I'm just worried about your health. I know this isn't you. My Darryn would never hit me. This is the drugs, and you need help, babe," Madetra told him compassionately.

"I don't need help; I just need you. I can kick my drug habit on my own, as long as you promise not to leave me." Darryn burst into tears while climbing off of her. "If you promise not to leave me, I promise, I'll never hit you again, and I promise I'll quit using."

"Baby, I'm not going to leave you," Madetra said, cradling him in her arms. "Whatever it is you're going through, we'll deal with it together. In sickness and in health, for better or for worse, till death do us part . . . remember?"

"Yeah, I remember, Mad," he said as he started rocking back and forth and crying like a baby. "I remember."

E'AN

E'an was preparing for a new client when he received a call from Madetra.

"I need your help, E'an. I have a patient that I think has a drug problem and he needs a good therapist. Do you know of anyone? And don't say you, because I would never subject anyone I cared about to you."

"So you can ask for my referrals but you can't refer me?"

"E'an, be for real. You know our history. Do I need to remind you about our ski trip?"

"Touché. I know of several great therapists. I have a late client on her way, and after I meet with her, I'll compose a list and e-mail it to you."

"Sounds great," Madetra said, struck by his sincerity and compassion for the first time since she had known him. Ever since she had threatened him that night at Lake Tahoe, E'an had started acting like a different person. "Thanks, E'an. I'll talk to you later."

Before he could spend any more time thinking about Madetra or her patient, E'an Shaw's two o'clock appointment appeared. He was surprised to see that it was Destanie from DAT Club. She had given the office manager, Natalie—the one who handled his schedule—a fake name.

From what he had seen on DAT Club's first two trips, he had diagnosed her as being both depressed and obsessed with Finesse Brown.

"Hi, Destanie," E'an greeted her. "I wasn't expecting you. Please sit down."

Destanie did as she was told. She felt bad about being late, but it wasn't entirely her fault. Kay and Finney were growing increasingly close, and she'd been following them around town all morning.

Heck, proper stalking took time.

"I'm sorry I'm late, and I'm sorry I gave your secretary a fake name. I wasn't sure if I was really even coming until this morning, so I didn't want to give out my real name."

"No need to apologize. Why don't we get started? Tell me why you're here."

After about five minutes with Destanie, E'an could tell his diagnosis was correct and that she was long overdue for therapy. "It's clear to me that you're depressed. And you have an unhealthy fixation on Finesse. You're beyond the point of being obsessed with him. It's classic. Textbook. If I were a betting man, I'd say your depression was triggered by the break-up of your relationship with Finesse."

"Depression and obsession? So, there's my diagnosis—short and sweet, huh?" she asked.

E'an felt sorry for Destanie. She seemed so defeated. It was official. She had a medical condition that could be looked up in a dictionary, written about in psychiatric journals, discussed on radio talk shows by self-appointed experts, joked about on inane, banal television sitcoms, and made into over-the-top movies.

"Since my craziness has a name, that means there must be a cure, right? Is there some pill or shot I can take to get rid of my problems? Because, let me tell you, being obsessed with someone who could care less whether you lived or died is no fun," she said with a laugh. It was a bitter, callous, menacing laugh. Okay, maybe it wasn't. Maybe it was just a plain old garden-variety laugh, but it spooked E'an all the same.

"You see, that's the problem with society—everyone wants a quick fix. They want to take this pill to lose weight, they want to apply that product to their faces to reduce wrinkles, they want to inject this product into their legs to break up cellulite. Well, I have a news flash for you— everything cannot be fixed so easily," he exclaimed with a little too much misplaced passion.

"So you're saying there is no pill or shot?"

He looked at her sympathetically. "No, there is no pill or shot."

"So what about treatment?"

"There are a couple of things we can do. Number one, I think we should continue with weekly psychotherapy sessions for thirty minutes. We may want to even increase your sessions from once a week to two or three times a week for at least a month. We may also want to go up to one hour. Secondly, I'm going to write you a prescription for some drugs. Serotonin reuptake inhibitors like Prozac, Paxil, or Zoloft could help."

"Okay."

As E'an wrote out her prescription, Destanie tried to fill the quiet with nervous chitchat. "Therapy, huh? Do you want me to talk about my childhood?"

"No," E'an said while handing her a prescription for Paxil.

"How about my deceased parents? My job? My weight problem? My friends or family? My ex? Kay? DAT Club?"

"No, no, no, no, no, and no. I don't mean to seem so detached, but people's ideas of therapy are so clichéd," E'an said as he watched her squirm. "We have plenty of time to talk about all of those things, particularly Finesse, but with me treating you, you'll find I'm a bit unorthodox. Coming to terms with your depression and obsessive tendencies is going to take time. We have to start with baby steps."

"Okay, what do we do first?"

"I want to start things off a little differently than most therapists would. I want us to begin each session with your very own personal positive affirmation statement. Please read this for me." He handed her a piece of paper, after rummaging through his desk. "Actually, why don't you sing it to the tune of 'Itsy Bitsy Spider'?" he suggested.

Destanie did as she was instructed.

"Depressed and obsessive, I can not be, because that ain't working, that don't work for me. Whenever I start to feel those awful tendencies, I need to change my behavior, that's really the key."

They stared at each other in silence when she was done.

E'an was very proud of his innovation, an adjunct to therapy that he'd come up with a few years ago. Between him, drugs and the "Itsy Bitsy Spider," it would only be a matter of time before Destanie would be cured.

For a fleeting moment he couldn't help wondering if the same treatment would've worked for his momma and her obsessive-compulsive behavior.

"I know what you just did may seem a little 'New Age,' but whenever you find things getting out of control, sing that. It will help you better internalize what you need to do to heal," E'an informed Destanie, not realizing that he seemed more unhinged than she did.

"Why sing it to the tune of 'Itsy Bitsy Spider'?" Destanie asked in bewilderment.

"It will give you something to think about. Everything we do is guided by one main philosophy of life. How do you look at situations that occur in your life? Is the glass half empty or half full? Are you an optimist or a pessimist?"

"What?" she asked, perplexed.

"Was the spider an optimist who was going to achieve his goal of getting up that spout no matter what? You know, if at first you don't succeed, try again. Or did you perceive the spider as a hard-headed, know-it-all that didn't know it was time to give up?"

"That's kind of deep," Destanie said, finally comprehending what he was saying. "How you view the spider is a reflection of how you view life, huh?"

"Exactly."

"Okay. I have a question for you, Doc. What do I

sing the next time I want to beat Kay into a bloody pulp or have sex with Finesse next to her dead body?"

E'an didn't have a nursery rhyme song for that.

"We'll deal with all of that in therapy, starting next week," he said without flinching. He'd heard a lot of crazy claims from patients, and what she had just said was tame compared to a lot of things he'd heard over the years.

"Okay," Destanie said, knowing full well that she wouldn't be coming back. It was obvious that neither E'an, the "Itsy Bitsy Spider," nor anyone else could save her from her destructive obsession with Finesse Brown.

"The best and most beautiful things in the world cannot be seen or even touched. They must be felt with the heart."
~ Helen Keller

MADETRA

Elbows and assholes.

There was no better way to describe the Freak-fest that was Hedonism III. While her husband and the men in DAT Club loved their newest vacation hot spot, Mad at first regretted that she'd been so quick to go along with DAT Club's decision to take their April trip to an *au naturel* beach resort on Jamaica's north coast.

While the resort's accommodations were nice and included two-person Roman tubs and over-the-bed mirrors in most rooms, not to mention a see-through slide that snaked through the disco, Mad just couldn't get used to seeing so many nude and not-so-attractive bodies in one place. No matter how many times she went to the beach, she was stunned by the fact that nearly all the guests wore little more than shades, smiles, and suntan oil.

Before the trip, she had never considered herself a prude, and she was a little surprised at how she now felt.

She looked at nude bodies all day long.

The more she thought about it, the more she realized E'an was the one responsible for her discomfort. While she had agreed from the very beginning to participate in whatever trips DAT Club as a whole decided to do, the last thing she was going to do was let her pervert sexual harasser see her naked.

When DAT Club arrived at the Hedonism III resort a few days ago, Mad's husband mysteriously disappeared during the days, and she only saw him at night when it was time for bed. Everyone else hung out well into the evenings as a group, and Madetra often found herself talking to, paired up with, or wandering off with Gerald, not that she was complaining about spending a lot of time with him.

Gerald was charming, warm, and attentive, just like her husband once was. He even, out of respect, for her did the "formal thing."

The two of them were the only two in the group who opted to wear swimsuits and cover-ups whenever DAT Club got together for activities like glass bottom boat cruises, swimming, kayaking, volleyball, shuffleboard, sailing, fishing, water skiing, snorkeling, parasailing, and hiking.

"Wake up! Earth to Madetra," a voice in the distance said.

Imagining at first that it belonged to Gerald, Madetra was a bit disappointed when she realized the voice was coming from her twin sister.

"Where's your mind at, girl? What's up with you? Am I gonna have to slap you today, Crazy?" Kay asked with her signature 'tude.

Bare breasts, buttocks, cocks, and cunts surrounded them as they made their way to their special spa treatment.

"I can't believe I let you talk me into getting a Brazilian bikini wax," Madetra complained. "I've never had one before."

"Who knows?—Your silly man might like it." Kay laughed. "I want to see you take a walk on the wild side, do something to loosen yourself up. Shoot! We all could stand to loosen up," Kay said.

"Not you. You're loose enough, Ms. Shake My Tail and Scuff My Stuff For Money."

"Yeah, but you're not. By the way, you're supposed to be nude, like yours truly," Kay reminded her as she threw her arms up in the air and struck a pose.

"I've got on a bikini, and this is as naked as I am going to get."

"All right, Sista Killjoy. We better hurry, or we'll miss our appointment," Kay, the always-late queen stated as she untied Mad's bikini top and ran with it down the hallway.

With her boobs exposed to God and everybody, Mad was mortified. She crossed her arms over her chest and ran down the hall after her laughing sister.

A few moments later, they arrived at their destination. During breakfast, they'd heard wonderful things about the on-site spa, and Kay immediately used Madetra's credit card to book treatments for them both.

"Hello, my name is Helga. Welcome to LaPlaz Spa for Women," a pretty, young, stout, blonde woman greeted them as they entered the spa breathless from running.

"We are Kaylantra Ellis and Madetra Price, here

for our four o'clock treatments," Kay responded in as refined a tone as she could muster in-between giggles.

"This way, please." Helga guided them through a maze of long, white, peaceful corridors that led to a huge Jacuzzi tub. "Ladies, soak in here for a while, and someone will be with you soon."

Kay jumped right in, but Madetra eyed the tub and her sister with disdain.

"Mad, you have got to hurry up and get in here. The water feels wonderful," Kay yelled.

"I ain't got to do nothin' but stay black and die," Mad mumbled aloud while walking toward the Jacuzzi, eyeing it as if it were a guillotine.

"Come on, slow poke."

"Why we are torturing ourselves?" Mad dipped her feet into the near-scalding water.

"This isn't torture, it's a treat. If you're going to be walking around nude all weekend, you might as well make sure you shower, shampoo, and shine. That's what this spa treatment is all about."

"I'm not planning on walking around this place naked with my stuff hanging out all weekend."

"To be honest, I'm surprised your crazy man would want to come on this trip."

"Speaking of my crazy man, I've hardly seen Darryn since we got here," Madetra told her. "During our Minnesota trip and our ski trip things were so great, and then things have been going downhill ever since. I think me confronting him about doing drugs and him hitting me may have had something to do with it."

"What? He hit you? He's doing drugs? Why haven't you said anything about this before now? I could have a crew from HOTGIRLZ beat him down. If my so-called man knocked the hell out of me because I asked him about some questionable mess he was doing, things would go downhill hella quick and I would be moving on. You need to tell him to kick rocks. Kick his sorry behind to the curb."

"It's not that easy, when you've been with someone since you were sixteen. I love Darryn. I'm not leaving him. I simply have to make him see he has a problem and needs help."

"While you're busy loving him, be prepared to get knocked on your ass a few more times. Don't be a stupid, naïve chick behind that no-good wife-beating asshole."

"He promised he wouldn't hit me again," Madetra said quietly.

"That's not even a sentence that should be coming out of your mouth. If you ask me—good riddance. You should be whooping and hollering over the fact that you haven't seen much of him during this trip."

"Kay, he is my husband of eleven years—"

"Whatever. He conveniently forgot that when he hit you, didn't he? Hmmm . . . forget him. You're grown and I ain't trying to raise you. Do what you feel you gotta do. I don't want to talk about his sorry behind no more. One person I do want to talk about is Gerald. I noticed he's been paying a lot more attention to you than your own husband."

"So you noticed?"

"Yep. What's up with you and Gerald? Every time the group gets together, the two of you somehow manage to wind up close."

"Gerald is so different from Darryn. If I weren't

married, I'd get with him in a heartbeat. He's so attentive and nice . . . plus, the man is packing. Have you seen the man in his swim trunks?" Madetra asked laughing.

"Yeah, I've seen him, but he doesn't compare to my baby. Oh, goodness! I can't believe how hard I've fallen for Finney."

"I can't believe it either. You're in love! I think that's great. But isn't Destanie making it hard on you two?"

"Forget about her. I can't imagine why she's still even a part of this group. Seeing us together I know is driving her crazy. It's about time for that psycho to leave him alone. Maybe if she sees we're serious, she'll move on."

"In your dreams. You can keep thinking that if you want to, but have you ever see the movie, *Fatal Attraction*?"

"That's her to a T," Kay said with a nervous laugh. "Did I tell you she leaves him cum messages all the time?"

"She leaves him cum what?"

"You don't even want to know."

Mad laughed. "You're right—I don't think I do. But don't let Desperate Destanie get to you. I'm just happy you're in love. There's a first time for everything, even for old folks like you."

"Let's change the subject. I don't want to jinx my relationship with Finesse."

"Okay, consider the subject changed. What do you want to talk about now?"

"E'an. Ever since you told me about him sexually harassing you, I've been watching him like a hawk. He's good; I haven't seen anything out of the ordinary."

"That's because he's tuned everything down. I confronted him in Tahoe. Threatened to sue him, and he's been acting like a totally different person. So, how's *your* harassment situation?"

"Eddie is as big a jerk as usual, and between him and this client on the job that I'm doing, I have my hands full."

"What do you mean? Does Finesse know you're having sex with him and two other men?"

"Uhmmm . . . no. I'm keeping myself protected, and if things continue to get serious between us, I'm going to give up both the stripping and the online site. I'll actually consider going legit."

"Wow! I never thought I'd live to hear you say that. Won't you miss old what's his name . . . Soul-Viewer . . . your online friend?"

Kay couldn't help but smile when she heard his name.

On more than one occasion, SoulViewer had tried to get Kay to give up her sexual online life.

He even offered to pay, anonymously of course, for her to go back to school—that is if she signed off of the Internet permanently.

"Yeah, I'll miss him. He's the only thing I'll miss about the online gig besides the money."

"Has he ever tried to meet you?"

"Nope, he's different from the others who have begged to meet me. I guess in his mind, what happens online stays online. But, we're jumping the gun. I said, *if* things continue to get serious with Finesse I'll quit. We have to see how that relationship shakes out first."

"Just don't do anything *else* to spoil it."

"Besides sleeping with two other men, what else could I do?" Kay asked with a nervous laugh. "So tell me, what are you dressing up as tonight for the masquerade party?" Kay asked.

"That's for me to know and you to find out. And speaking of that masquerade party, I don't suppose there is any way I can actually get out of going, is there?"

"Not if you want to live!" Kay said as she grabbed Madetra's leg and pulled her underneath the water's surface.

"Kay, watch the 'do! It just got done."

"Sorry. This water is so relaxing," she whispered as she closed her eyes and sunk deeper.

"Well, it's making me feel like a prune. I'm going for my massage. Are you coming?" Mad asked while climbing out of the hot tub.

"Nope, not yet. I'm going to hang out here for a little while longer."

"Fine. Suit yourself," Mad said as she grabbed a white robe from the closet behind them.

"Mrs. Price, what are you doing out of the hot tub?" Helga asked when she saw Madetra wandering aimlessly in the spa's main lobby a few moments later.

"I'm not really in the mood for the hot tub today," Mad explained. "Do you think I can use those extra minutes for a longer massage?"

"Absolutely, whatever you would like." Helga guided Madetra into a small, room decorated in muted tones, located at the back of the spa. The room contained a massage table, a few framed pictures of peaceful nature scenes, shelves full of good-smelling lotions and oils, and a small boom box playing a tape of nature sounds.

"Ummm, bubbling brook—my favorite," Mad

said aloud as she discarded her robe and climbed up on the massage table.

Once her masseuse stepped in, Madetra pointed out her trouble spots and, within minutes, was fast asleep. She woke up an hour later and got a facial, manicure, and pedicure before meeting Kay in the lobby.

"What? No bikini? Ohhhhh . . . look at you. Somebody's feeling herself, huh? You're looking all naked and lovely—almost look as good as me," Kay teased.

"I almost look as good as you? Hmmm . . . screw you, Kay!"

"Speaking of screwing, I gotta go see a man about a horse. I gotta go see my honey about something to ride."

"Your euphemisms suck, you freak!" Madetra said with a laugh. "Tell Finesse I said hi. I'll see you both tonight at the party."

"We'll be there. See ya," Kay said with a smile as she left Madetra behind to pay for their treatments.

FINESSE

Life was good. *Hell! Life was great.* The love of a good woman could always make a man feel that way. Yep, Finesse was in love; there was no question about it. Kay said she loved him too, and her love was nothing like the depressing, controlling, obsessive love that Destanie had for him.

"You ready to go again?" Kay asked, interrupting his thoughts.

He smiled at the memory of their most recent sexual encounter. The minute he saw her gorgeous nude body walk through the door after she got back from the spa, he literally pushed her against the wall, lifted her, and made love to her.

She went along with the program by immediately pouring on the sex compliments. She had him out there, feeling like a king. He loved the way it felt inside her, loved the way she moved, loved the way she smiled right before she came against that wall. It drove him out of his head—the way she kissed him and whispered what she wanted him to do to her. He nibbled her shoulder, grabbed her bottom, and spread her cheeks. He nearly drove them both crazy when he softly stroked her and teased her by dipping the tip of his manhood slowly in and out of her.

Her mouth whispered that she hated being teased. She said it was just plain rude and drove her nuts, even though her body said otherwise.

After they climaxed together, she rubbed his love juice all over her stomach and breasts. She told him she did it so she could feel his warmth, his essence.

When he heard that, it turned him on and had him wanting her again. He was intoxicated by the sense of power she so casually held over him. He carried her in his arms over to the couch and manhandled her doggy-style. He strummed her clit hard and fast and drove himself inside her from behind with increasing frequency and force. Her moans and screams of pleasure guided him to a sexual summit that he'd only dreamed of.

At the moment when the surge of his love began flowing through the inner walls of her vagina, she clamped her thighs together tightly and held her breath, allowing the waves of her orgasm to pass through them both.

Finesse felt lucky.

He had always managed to find women that knew how to throw it on him, and Kaylantra was far and away better than anyone he had ever been with. Even crazy Destanie.

"What if I told you I wanted to stay in tonight and do the 'hokie poke-me' all night long?" Kay asked.

"You've been talking about the party all day. You sure you want to miss it?"

"No, I don't want to miss it. Okay, okay, we're going to the party, but this is so nice, I don't want it to end."

"It doesn't have to," Finesse told her. "Tell me a little more about this hokie poke-me thing; better yet, show me."

"Bring El Largo over here, and I will," Kay said while reaching for his love stick.

"My momma always warned me about you midwestern girls. Said you ain't got nothing to do but lay in the cornfields daydreaming about men all day."

"Your mother is just as crazy as you are, apparently. So tell me about her. Do you think she will approve of me?"

"Probably not," he answered honestly. "She never thinks anyone is good enough for her baby—that's why I'm glad she's on the East Coast; she doesn't ever get to meet my girlfriends."

"Do you think I'm good enough for you?"

"Would I be here if I didn't? The truth is, I want even more with you; when we get home, I want you to move in with me."

His words stunned her. "Really? Are you sure?"

Ever since their shared Mozzarella cheese-flavored kiss, they'd been an item—but not even Kay realized how deeply Finesse had fallen for her.

"Yep, but you'd have to go legit. I don't want strange men getting a peek at what I'm poking."

"Okay, that's not exactly a marriage proposal, but it's a helluva good start," Kay said laughing.

"So we're going to be roomies?"

"Yep. And regarding what you were saying about your momma not thinking I'm good enough for you, I think all parents think that about their children. That's what I'm guessing. I remember that about my parents before they died. People thought I was fast, my parents included, but I wasn't. I just remember both my mom and dad telling me that I needed to watch myself. They told me not everyone deserved me because I had gold between my legs."

Finney laughed. "They actually said that to you? Your parents had the nerve to say that to you? No wonder you got issues!"

"Yep, they said it." Kay nodded vigorously. "They sure did! I'm 24-karat gold, baby—didn't you know?"

He laughed again. "That's gonna be my name for you—24-karat. Why don't you give me a new name? I hate El Largo."

"I know. All men walk around thinking they're big, but with that name you don't have to think it . . . you know it! Besides, it's better than Heaven, Willard, Taco, Brains, Thursday, and Mr. Weiner, ain't it?"

" 'Mr. Weiner'?"

"Don't ask."

"Look at you. You're a stripper, yet you've only slept with seven men, including me. I feel special. In today's day and age, it's like you're almost a virgin."

"On what planet am I almost a virgin? Planet Screw-A-Lot?"

He laughed. "Yep, now there's a town I could be mayor of."

"I don't even want to know about all the women you've been with. I bet that's scary. I know all I need to know. We've had HIV tests and every other kind of STD test done and we're both clean."

"Well, come bring your clean behind on over

here, 24-karat and let's do the hokie poke-me at least one more time before tonight's party."

"You read my mind," Kay said as she reached for him, ushering his hardness inside of her with a smile.

"If you come to a fork in the road, take it."
~ Yogi Berra

GERALD

Talk about your freaks!

The masquerade party, which was outside behind the hotel, was off the chain! The promotional materials about the resort bragged about the weekend masquerade parties, so people came prepared.

Half of the people at the fete were naked, wearing only masks and smiles. The other half were wearing costumes that revealed a peek into their favorite sexual fantasies. Booze poured freely. Food was in abundance. Folks were getting their freak on in plain view, and for those not having sex, the promise of lovemaking hovered in the air.

The built-in anonymity of the evening gave women the courage to walk around the grounds dressed as Catholic schoolgirls, French maids, nurses, prostitutes, cavewomen, sexpots, and naughty nuns, boosting men's egos and sniffing their jocks.

Dressed in costumes ranging from flashers, pirates, cavemen and robots to vampires, priests, princes, pimps, and everything in-between—the men talked to every woman that boldly stepped to them and to women that they themselves boldly stepped to, including those who pretended that they didn't want to be bothered.

The joint was buzzing about some of the entertainment and contests planned for the evening. There was going to be an erotic poetry "slam jam," "erotic password," "naked twister," strip card games, and arousing games of musical beds, and limbo. And, of course, there were going to be contests that judged body parts and all things sexual!

Gerald had seen a lot of things in his brief twenty-seven years on earth, but he had never seen anything like what he saw that weekend when DAT Club went to Jamaica. After a while he had become numb to all the exposed body parts. The idea of seeing yet another pair of breasts or another bald or hairy mound didn't appeal to him in the least.

Okay, that wasn't entirely true—there was one mound and one pair of breasts that he was dying to see, but she belonged to someone else.

Gerald walked around in full pimp gear along with E'an and Destanie, who were both dressed as vampires. "Who are you looking for all hot and heavy?" Destanie asked as she stuck her ever-present mini news camera in Gerald's face.

"I'm not looking for anyone," he lied, unable to hide the irritation in his voice as they made their way through the scantily dressed crowd.

He didn't understand how he'd managed to get stuck with E'an and Destanie, but he tried to make the best out of an awful situation. He personally couldn't stand Destanie because she was obviously stalking Finney and Kay. She and Finesse had been covering the DAT Club trips for the news and he knew for her that had to be hard. He knew personally how hard it was to watch the love of your life love someone else, and he just didn't understand how Destanie could do it. Heck, he was struggling with the same problem himself!

He also personally couldn't stand E'an because E'an wanted Madetra, but since he was a firm believer in the idiom—you should keep your friends close and your enemies closer—he didn't complain when E'an asked if he wanted to hang out at the party. There was only one person Gerald really wanted to hang out with—Madetra Price—his personal Florence Nightingale.

Earlier during the day, while the group was parasailing, although Madetra mentioned that she was coming to the masquerade party, he didn't put it past her to change her mind. She had even talked about coming to the party with Finesse, her sister, and her husband. Gerald really hoped that she would be there and that, if she did come, she wouldn't bring Darryn. He doubted seriously that her husband could show up even if he wanted to.

The last time Gerald saw him, Darryn was strung out, begging him for more coke. Convincing him to get his drugs from Gerald while they were in Lake Tahoe was easy. It had also been easy to get him hooked on harder stuff when they first arrived in Jamaica a few days before. It had all been so easy, in fact, that he almost felt sorry for Madetra, but he knew he had to stay the course. He was determined to win her at all costs—even if that included the drug-induced death of her husband.

Despite the fact that plenty of women came on to him, after about an hour, Gerald was ready to leave the party—until he saw Madetra. While she was wearing a mask like everyone else, he knew it was her the instant he saw her. She was dressed as a sexy French maid. How could he not recognize her when he'd memorized every curve of her body, every nod of her head, every lilt in her step?

As he walked toward Madetra with E'an following closely behind him, Gerald noticed that she was with her sister and Finesse. Kay was dressed as a Get Christie Love-like prostitute, and Finney was dressed as her pimp. There were no signs of Madetra's husband, Darryn.

Just to mess with her, Gerald pulled down his mask and decided to flirt. He stepped to her as one of his favorite, old, slow songs, Maxwell's "Whenever, Wherever, Whatever" started blasting through oversized speakers. When Gerald stretched out his hand for her to join him on the dance floor, he could tell she was going to initially blow him off with the old "I don't slow-dance with strangers" line. But then she looked deep into his eyes, saw the man behind the mask, and grabbed his hand.

Wrestling to fight a growing attraction that they dared not speak into existence, they danced together for the rest of the evening without either of them saying a word.

Without words they could pretend that they didn't know each other. They could pretend that they were strangers without any attachments to one another. They could pretend that what they were thinking and doing and feeling wasn't wrong.

*   *   *   *   *   *   *

The next morning, the members of DAT Club, with the exception of Destanie, got together for breakfast.

"There's my boy, Gerald," E'an said as Gerald approached the group.

"So did you have a good time last night? Did you have fun at the masquerade party?" Kay asked.

"Did you? What were you dressed as? What kind of costume did you have on?" Gerald asked innocently.

"Don't play," Kay said laughing. "You know exactly what I was wearing and what everyone else at this table was wearing."

"You got me confused with some other man. I don't think I saw anyone here at this table last night," he lied.

Kay threw a few peanuts at him. "Whatever."

"Hey, watch it, I'm allergic to peanuts," he told her. "So did everyone have fun last night?"

"Yep. Too bad you didn't see me—I was looking hot," Kay said with a lopsided smile. "And so was my sister."

"Hmmm . . . too bad I didn't see you," Gerald teased.

"You wouldn't have had to see Kay, you could hear her big mouth a mile away," Darryn joked.

"Forget you, Darryn!" Kay shot back. "By the way, I'm surprised to see you even down here for breakfast. Where have you been? We haven't peeped you much since we got here."

"Where I have been is none of your business," he said, unable to make eye contact with anyone in the group. "I actually have been leaving early in the morning to find secluded spots on the island so I can get some work done without distractions, and when I return, I just go straight to the room and camp out there to eat and sleep."

"It's called a vacation for a reason—you need to try spending more time with your woman and less time with those numbers," Kay scolded.

"The next time I want your advice, I'll make sure I ask for it. Mad, business calls. I'm going up to the room to do some work. If I'm not there when you come in, it's probably because I needed a change of scenery and went to work somewhere else," Darryn announced before abruptly leaving the group.

Kay rolled her eyes at him the whole time he was talking and mumbled under her breath. "Blah, blah, blah."

"Kay babe . . . you need to let him handle his," Finney whispered in her ear. "Stay out of his business and stay out of your sister's."

Kay rolled her eyes at him, got up, and headed back to the buffet line with her man right behind her.

"As you can see, it's been a kind of crazy morning. Everybody's nerves are on edge," Madetra told Gerald. "Before you came down, Destanie was here—"

"Awww, that was some funny mess," E'an said, interrupting them.

Gerald asked, "What was so funny? What happened?"

"Finney and Kay announced they were moving in together," Madetra told him, "and Destanie immediately burst into tears."

"She said she couldn't fathom spending a morning watching the two of them celebrating the fact that they'd be shacking up and living in sin, and then she split," E'an elaborated.

"Can you believe that?" Madetra asked.

"Noooo!" Gerald said in mock horror. "She actually used the word *fathom*?"

E'an and Gerald burst into laughter.

"You're both crazy and insensitive jerks," Madetra chastised them.

"In my defense, I *am* a little hung-over from last night," E'an said, "and for that very reason, I think I need to return to my room and go lay down."

As they watched him walk away, Madetra and Gerald shared a smile. "Do you always clear out a room this fast?" she asked. "You hungry? You want some of my pancakes?"

"Nope. I see those chopped nuts on top. Didn't you just hear me mention earlier that I'm allergic to nuts, especially peanuts? If I eat that, within minutes, I'll be one big spastic welt knocking on death's door. I'll just have some OJ." He poured himself a glass.

"So you never answered your own question— did you have fun at the party?"

"I had a blast. I danced with this fine specimen of a woman for most of the night. She kind of reminded me of you."

"Hmmm, I danced with a man most of the night that was pretty special too."

"So . . . did anything exciting happen between the two of you? Did you kiss him? Did you have sex with him?" Gerald asked, already knowing the answers.

Madetra nearly gagged on her pancakes. "Dang! It's like that? You're being kind of vulgar and crass, aren't you? No, I didn't have sex with him. I'm married, remember?"

"Okay, you two, what's the plan for today?" Kay asked as she and Finesse returned to their seats. "We're going gambling. You want to join us?"

"I'm in," Gerald said. "I'll see if E'an wants to go too. When are you going?"

"In a couple of hours."

"Count me out. I'm going to try to spend some time with my workaholic husband. I'm going to see if he can't take just a little break from work. I'll see you all when you get back," Madetra said sadly before heading in the direction of her room.

MADETRA

"Psssst, Mr. St. John," Madetra shouted as she stared at Gerald's head below her balcony. "Psssst, Mr. St. John."

Gerald St. John looked up and happily waved some cheddar at her. "Guess who just won a few ducats?"

"Come on up, let's celebrate," she told him.

Within a matter of minutes, Gerald was knocking on Madetra's door.

Once she opened the door, he rushed in, speaking a thousand words a minute. "I just won a grand playing black jack. Can you believe it? I never have that kind of luck! This kind of stuff never happens to me! Never!"

His excitement was contagious and intoxicating as he rambled on and on about winning his money.

An excitement deep within Madetra grew too. The excitement was so strong that it surprised even her—especially when she found herself kneeling on the floor in front of him with her face in his groin.

Her hot breath near his member, gently, yet quickly, coaxed him to arousal.

"Whoa, Doc! What up? Whatchoo doin'? Where's your husband?" Gerald asked with a trace of a smile tugging at his soft, tender lips.

"He's in the next room," she teased. "I'm kidding—who knows where Darryn is? Let's concentrate on where we are. I want to help you celebrate your winnings," she told him as she successfully tugged down his shorts, only to be met by all 9 glorious inches of his long, stiff love pole.

"Wow! A full salute. I'm impressed. I look at men's anatomies all day long, an occupational hazard or blessing, depending on how you look at it, and if I'm not mistaken, I'd say you measure from my wrist to my elbow. So that's going to be my nickname for you."

"What? You're gonna call me wrist to elbow?" he asked with a laugh. "That's kind of awkward and long, ain't it?"

"No, silly. I'm going to call you My WE."

"I've had a lot of names, but that one ranks up there as one of the oddest. But you can call it whatever you want." He looked down and locked eyes with hers.

She stared at his face awhile and then turned her undivided attention back to his manhood. His shaft was hard and stiff, and like a magnet, she was drawn to it. She planted small kisses and nibbles on his head and then circled the ridge of his hard tool with her tongue.

She immediately heard moans well up from that

place of passion deep inside of him as she repeatedly licked him up one side of his shaft and down the other like it was her favorite flavor of ice-cream sitting proudly atop an ice-cream cone.

As she pleasured him, his moans grew louder and louder, fueling her desire to take him to higher and higher heights. The more he moaned, the more she desperately wanted to worship him, the more she desperately wanted to feel every inch of his warmth, every beat of his throbbing manhood.

Eager to please him, she glided her lips over his head and twirled her tongue all around his rod. She took him deeper and deeper down her throat, faster and faster, in and out of her mouth. She fed off his sounds, his feel, his taste, his smell and couldn't wait for his growing passion to erupt.

Faster, faster, faster; deeper, deeper, deeper.

Madetra took him in and out of her mouth and stroked him with her hand, totally in sync. She felt his meaty, flesh swell, thanks to the soft, wet moistness of her mouth. That made her happier than a thousand glorious Sundays.

She'd always liked the way Gerald St. John made her feel, and she wanted to return the favor.

Young. Flirty. Attractive. Healthy. Smart. Sexy. Desirable. She hadn't felt that way in ages with her husband. Not since the ski trip. In bed and out, her husband made her feel old, tired, and put upon.

As she expertly worked Gerald over, Madetra couldn't help but wonder if her husband would be pleased with how she'd retained all that he'd taught her. She refocused and turned her attention back to the young man whose pulsating member was in her mouth.

Loving Gerald St. John would be so easy, she thought.

Loving him would include lots of hot and sexy nights, deep conversations, no accusations or anger or daily reminders of regrets. Only adoration and respect. Only laughter and love. Only goodness and light. Thinking about really loving Gerald turned her on and made her want to pull out every weapon she had in her oral sex arsenal, but just as she was about to truly blow his mind, he gently pulled himself out of her mouth.

"We're getting carried away. You don't have to do that, Doc," he said quietly.

"I know I don't have to—I want to."

"Why? Why do you want to? I should be serving you. You deserve to be loved, pampered, and adored . . . behind closed doors. If you were mine, I'd treat you like the Nubian Queen you are. You're intriguing. The most fascinating, amazing, beautiful, and accomplished woman I know."

"Hmmm . . . it looks like someone is really feeling me."

"More than you know. Why do you think I'm always following you around like some little puppy dog? It's because I want to see you and spend time with you. No, let me correct that—it's because I *need* to see you and spend time with you. And the truth is I've really wanted to be with you since the night of the party, if not before."

A whole mix of emotions raced across Mad's face: nervousness, fear, and then an optimistic kind of happiness, an expectant unparalleled joy. She smiled. She felt exactly the same way that Gerald did. She had long suspected that Gerald St. John had a crush on her, but it made her feel good to finally hear him admit it.

"Man, I love your smile, and I love knowing I

put it there on your face," he said. "I'd like to put one there permanently, if you'd let me."

"Gerald, you know I'm married . . . there's no chance—"

"Don't even mention your marriage or your husband to me. You've got it going on, and why he isn't here appreciating every lovely, luscious inch of you is beyond me. You deserve so much more than what he gives you. You deserve better than him."

Tears gathered in her eyes. Madetra couldn't remember the last time a man seemed to genuinely care that much about her and her feelings. "So exactly what do I deserve, Mr. St. John?" she asked, hoping that she didn't sound too needy.

"Let me show you," he whispered.

They shared a look that touched her soul as he stretched out his hand.

She'd never before cheated on her husband, but since she felt so disconnected from the man she was married to, what was wrong with having an affair? If she was lucky, maybe like Stella, she'd get her groove back. No one would ever have to know about it, not even her sister. What happened between the two of them could stay just between the two of them.

Madetra reached out to grab Gerald's hand and her blessing. Unfortunately for her, as she did so, Madetra didn't notice that someone, somewhere from a balcony across the courtyard, was watching her every move and taking pictures of her sexual transgressions—for which there would later be hell to pay.

"To get through the hardest journey, we need take only one step at a time, but we must keep on stepping."
~ Chinese proverb

DARRYN

When he returned from Jamaica, Darryn had to admit that he was not the same man he once was. His addiction had turned him into someone he no longer recognized. Things had not gone well there. He pretty much just stayed out of everyone's way and spent the majority of his time getting high. Luckily, when he ran out of his stash, Gerald always seemed to be there, ready to feed him what he needed.

Darryn needed to desperately fight his addiction, but he didn't even know where to start. He refused to see the therapist Madetra had told him about. He lied and told his wife he could stop the addiction cold turkey on his own.

Wanting desperately to believe him, she was waiting . . . watching . . . but it would all be in vain.

He couldn't stop. He didn't see his downward spiral ending any time soon. Luckily for him, he knew he had Madetra for life; she had too much history with him to just throw it all away. But watching him turn into a shell of a man was breaking her heart. Her disappointment in him oozed from every pore of her body. He was now more introverted than ever and was always in full-out liar mode. Most recently, he'd been lying to his wife about the stereo she'd just bought him. He told her that it wasn't working properly and that he had to send it back to be repaired. The reality was he pawned it because he needed money for his vices. After awhile, Mad stopped asking him when it would be fixed and returned. She knew the truth. He could tell. He could see it in her eyes. He could hear it in her voice. He could feel it deep down from within her very core whenever they tickled each other's privates.

While Madetra showered and he readied himself for work, Darryn could barely look at himself in the mirror. He had changed so much. He had long since let himself go when it came to his physical appearance.

His skin was no longer a smooth, heavenly brown—it was instead now dotted with pockmarks, pimples, scrapes, and bruises. He let his hair grow out and half the time didn't comb it and he had a mass of unsightly ingrown hair bumps. Plus, he lost more than 20 pounds during the course of the year—and he was slim to begin with. On top of that, he was irritable and grumpy and had developed a quick-trigger temper.

The way he dressed himself now was atrocious. He rarely dressed himself in anything other than sweat suits, jeans and T-shirts. He now only dressed up when he went to work, but even then, he never really looked pulled together like he used to. He now always looked wrinkled and unkempt. He no longer cared about designer labels and the newest fall fashions. He no longer took subscriptions to *Maxim* and *Men's Health*. A man who had once been so particular about his appearance, now no longer cared about how he looked.

He'd become a joke in the workplace. A functioning addict—that's what he heard one of his accounting colleagues call him recently. He wasn't nearly as sharp on the job as he used to be.

The plum consulting jobs that he used to manage were now given out to everyone but him—he was basically an errand boy—a pencil sharpener with legs.

His boss no longer trusted him or relied on him, and Darryn found he had to work longer hours to do half the work he did when he was at the top of his game. He hated what he had become.

He was working late and then partying early into the morning every day and on weekends. All he wanted to do was go out. He kept telling himself he was going through an early mid-life crisis. He had the nerve to blame it on his loving wife, who now barely spoke to him and avoided him as often as she could. In his mind, since they'd married so young, he never got to experience the partying life that most men in their twenties get to experience, so he was making up for it now.

Over the past nine months, he'd spent over forty thousand dollars on drugs, booze, and partying. The folks he started hanging out with at the clubs were always giving him something to snort, shoot, smoke, swallow, or inhale, and he took it all—no questions asked.

He even earned a nickname behind that mess—"Trash Man." Now look at the Trash Man. He was trashed with no idea of how he was going to get out of the mess he was in.

KAYLANTRA

They'd been back from Jamaica for two weeks, and it was time for Kay to move. She was ecstatic about moving into Finney's home and was thankful her sister and Gerald were helping her. Over the years she'd accumulated tons of stuff and didn't try to weed any of that out before moving. Luckily, Finesse was a patient man and didn't complain much as her move-in day turned into a move-in weekend.

"So are you happy to be moving in with me?" Finney asked as Kay stared in frustration at the mess in the back of his SUV.

"Happy doesn't even begin to describe how I feel. Are you sure you're ready for this? It's a pretty big step, us living together. You want to take back your offer yet?"

"Not in a million years."

"So what do the folks at the station think about you shacking up with a stripper and online porn operator?"

"The men cheer me on every day!" he said with a laugh. "Speaking of your jobs, do you remember what we talked about?"

"How could I forget? You're expecting me to go legit. I'm quitting HOTGIRLZ, and I'm also closing down alwayshot&ready.com."

"I really do expect you to do that, Kay. Have you figured out a timeline on when that will happen?"

"Finney, do I have to rush? I make excellent money. That kind of cheddar is going to be hard for me to make doing a nine-to-five."

"I know that, babe, but you have me to take care of you now."

"I don't need you to take care of me. I've been taking care of myself ever since I was sixteen; I'm used to it. I guess I'll try to quit at the end of the summer. Hopefully in four months, I'll have found a suitable gig."

"That's just it—you don't need another gig."

"Finney, let me do me, okay? I'm not going to just sit around here and let you take care of me. I have to bring in my own bank. That's just how I roll. End of the summer, I promise."

"Okay," he agreed, relieved. "You quit at the end of the summer, whether you have another job or not." He kissed her on her forehead before leaving.

"What was that about?" Madetra asked. "You two looked mighty serious."

"Finney expects me to go legit by the end of the summer."

"Hmmm . . . I'll believe that when I see it."

"Don't start. Thanks for helping me move by the way. I couldn't have done it without you and your boy, Gerald."

"Isn't he the cutest thing?" Madetra asked as she grinned from ear to ear.

"I'm not even going to ask if you've been doing him—that's obvious!" Kay told her as the two of them hugged each other and laughed.

"Ohhh . . . now that I have dirt on you, I need a favor. Finney said it looks like acid was leaked all across my front end some kind of way last night. I'm guessing that heifer, Destanie had something to do with it. You can believe I'll be confronting her ass about this shit and suing her in small claims if she confesses to doing anything! Although, to be honest, she did me a favor. My 10-year-old Cavalier was on its last legs anyway. The car is shot, and I need a rental until I can get to a dealership to buy something new. Since my credit sucks, I'm going to need you to get me a rental, and I'll need you to co-sign on a loan for me—think you can do that for your older sister?"

"You're only older by five minutes," Madetra said with a laugh. "And shouldn't your man be doing stuff like that for you?"

"I'm just moving in with him. I'm not asking him to do anything for me right off the bat. He already has that 'I'll-take-care-of-you' thing working my nerves."

"All right. I'll help your old ass out. Your whip is whipped, huh?"

"Beyond whipped."

"Okay, I can take you to a rental place this afternoon after we finish around here."

"Cool."

"Kay, there's something I have to tell you. I'm disbanding DAT Club. Our next trip will be our last."

"Why, girl?"

"It hasn't helped with my marriage; in fact, it's made things worse. My husband is addicted to drugs now, and from what I can see, he isn't having a whole lot of success trying to stop his addiction. Plus, I'm having an affair with a man outside of my marriage. And did I mention that traveling with my sexual harasser isn't a barrel of laughs?"

"I thought E'an chilled out after the second trip."

"He did, both around the office and on the trips, but still, I have this funny vibe when it comes to him. It's like he's always watching me. I feel like he's always up to something. He just creeps me out."

"Forget E'an! As long as he's cut out that sexual harassment nonsense, don't worry about him."

"That's easier said than done."

"So what about Darryn and the drugs? I'm sure he thinks he can stop cold turkey, but he most likely won't be able to. I see that mess at the club all the time—people claiming that they're fighting their addictions on their own, when in fact they're doing nothing but falling deeper and deeper into the addiction."

"I know he needs professional help, but he is determined to fight this on his own. I feel like all I can do is support him on whatever decision he makes."

"Is he making any progress fighting it on his own?"

"Nope."

"You could be a little more proactive, you know. Hell . . . drag his ass to a Drugs Anonymous meeting."

"I know. I could do more, but a part of me resents Darryn. I feel like he got himself into this mess and he needs to get himself out."

"That's a risky attitude to have, sis."

"I know. I didn't say it made a lot of sense, but I can't help how I feel right now."

"You aren't thinking straight because of Gerald."

"That could be."

"Well, DAT Club may not have helped you strengthen your marriage, but it was the best thing that ever happened to me. If it hadn't been for you, I would never have met Finney, and I would have never fallen in love with such a quality man."

"Thank me if you're still together in a year," Mad said with a laugh.

"Oh, we will be! We're going to be together a long, long time! You can believe that," Kay shot back while failing to notice a fully disguised, fully enraged, Destanie driving by in a non-descript, dark rental car that reeked of acid.

"I am going away where I shall have no past and no name, and where I shall be born again with a new face and an untried heart."
~ Sidonie Gabrielle

MADETRA

There was something bittersweet about DAT
Club's trip to Las Vegas, Madetra thought as
she lay in bed. It was August—the group's one-year
anniversary—and it would be their last trip. As
Madetra had explained to Kay, she was disbanding
the group for personal reasons. The night before
the Vegas outing, she e-mailed everyone, to let
them know this would be the group's last trip together. Not surprisingly, no one responded, an in-
dication to Madetra that she'd made the right
decision.

Personally, the travel club fell far short of its intended goal—helping Madetra improve her life.
The group had fallen apart. E'an made her uncomfortable. She was having an extramarital affair.
Her husband was hooked on drugs, and her sister
and her boyfriend were being stalked and harassed by a crazy woman. Heck, if the trip hadn't
already been paid for in full, Madetra would have
long ago cancelled the Vegas excursion.

During the trip, every member of DAT Club had a room at the Bellagio, a grand hotel that paid homage to the art and architecture of northern Italy and southern France. Madetra picked the Bellagio because she loved the 1,000 fountains in front of the hotel that shot water 240 feet into the air in a highly synchronized fashion to the backdrop of opera and Italian music.

She also loved looking at the van Goghs, Monets, Renoirs, and Picassos hanging in the gallery, and the breathtaking display of 2,000 hand-blown glass flowers hanging from the lobby ceiling. And it went without saying that she was impressed by the hotel's upscale boutiques, which included Armani, Chanel, Gucci, Tiffany, Moschino, and Prada.

While looking out the window of her deluxe-sized hotel room, Madetra admired the amazing view of the Las Vegas Strip, Lake Bellagio, and the mountains.

So much had happened since DAT Club had started, some of it good and some of it bad. Madetra smiled as she thought of the good. She had fallen in love—*technically that was bad—but the way Gerald made her feel was good.* She didn't know what the future would hold for the two of them, especially since she was a woman who believed in making her marriage work, no matter what.

She tried to tell herself that Gerald was just for the moment, a temporary, five-month distraction. But saying it and believing it were two different things. They'd been together sexually, mentally, physically, and every other way every day, since that fateful trip to Jamaica.

How she had allowed herself to fall in love with Gerald in the first place still stupefied her. She was supposed to be the "good" sister. She was the one that put everyone else first—her sister, her husband, her patients—but with Gerald it felt as if she was finally putting herself first.

He was attractive, attentive, smart, funny, good in bed, and he made her feel special. Since that first time they were together in Jamaica, she had memorized his scent.

Not a day went by where she didn't yearn to kiss him or feel him beside her, inside her. Everything about him was indelibly etched on her heart and had been for a long while.

Gerald was definitely one bad habit that Madetra was finding hard to break, but she knew she had to give him up cold turkey—and soon—because she belonged to someone else. She'd been married for years. She was in love with her husband.

Till death us do part? Wasn't that the commitment she made before God, family, friends, and Darryn?

Just thinking about her drug-addicted husband hurt Madetra to her very core. She'd seen men addicted to drugs, like Darryn, at the clinic all the time. She knew her husband was in trouble, but instead of trying to save him, Madetra allowed another man in their marriage. She was relying on someone else to save *her*.

She reflected for a brief moment on her and Gerald and smiled. She then glanced at the nearby alarm clock and jumped out of bed with thoughts of her weekend planted firmly in her head. It was nine. Her husband had been gone for a while, and she was glad to have the hotel room to herself because Gerald was on his way.

She had scheduled way more activities than DAT Club could possibly do in one weekend. First, around noon they were going on a tour of Hoover Dam. She couldn't wait to explore this national historic landmark and engineering wonder of the world. She was excited about venturing down to the observation room in the power plant to view the massive generators. Just the idea of being so close to such an amazing body of water thrilled the swimmer in her.

From there, they'd be going to the "touristy" Grand Canyon and they planned to visit the Valley of Fire State Park to view millions of years of natural land erosion in pastel colors, and jutting rock formations in the mountains surrounding the area. Madetra had heard the view was awe-inspiring and, in many ways, almost spiritual.

Then over the course of the weekend they were going to visit Madame Tussaud's Interactive Attraction, a 300,000-square-foot, two-story wax museum that immortalized in wax, figures from the past and present worlds of film, sports, and music. There were over 100 featured celebrity images, and Madetra couldn't wait to see the lifelike wax figures of some of her favorite entertainers, including Elvis, J-Lo, George Clooney, the Rat Pack, and African-American sports figures like Tiger Woods, Evander Holyfield, Shaq, and Ali.

DAT Club was also going to check out one of the theatrical shows from *Cirque du Soleil* at MGM Grand. Madetra had read reviews about the dazzling live event. The show combined acrobatic performances, martial arts, puppetry, and pyrotechnics, to illustrate the nature of duality.

The breathtaking production was an epic tale

about two separated twins, who embark on very individualistic journeys to fulfill their destinies. Because it was about twins, it really piqued Madetra's interest, reminding her of her own twin, who, since getting with Finesse, now seemed like a totally different and happy person.

The group also planned to take helicopter rides over the city so they could view some of Vegas' legendary landmarks on The Strip. And they wanted to also get a taste of the city's black heritage, so they were going to visit attractions like downtown's Stewart Street, the Left of Center Gallery, and the Nevada State Museum.

Finally, they were of course, planning on doing some serious gambling and they were going to check out live entertainment shows like those of Celine Dion, George Wallace, David Copperfield, Jay Leno, Gladys Knight, and Frankie Beverly & Maze.

Just the thought of all they were going to try to do over the course of the weekend made Madetra smile. She was happy, healthy, and loved. What more could she want—other than for the person that she loved to be her husband?

She knew what she really wanted. She knew what she had to do. She had to stop being selfish and step up; she had to re-dedicate herself to her marriage and her husband; and she had to stop living in the fantasy world she'd created with Gerald. It was finally time.

* * * * * * *

"Are you ready?" Gerald asked as he knocked on Mad's door thirty minutes later.

"Not exactly," she said as she opened the door in the buff.

"What a great way to say hello. You better watch it, or I'm going to expect this kind of greeting all the time."

"About that . . ."

"What? I don't like the way that sounds."

"Gerald, we need to talk," Madetra said sadly as she ushered him into her suite.

She sat sullenly on one end of the sofa, and he sat beside her. She had to finally do the right thing and with any luck, it would be one helluva good-bye.

"You know, when you and I hooked up in Jamaica, things were kind of crazy for me. My husband was missing in action, my sister announced she was moving in with a guy she barely knew, and I needed to deal with some stuff that I wasn't quite ready to deal with. At the time that we hooked up, I just needed a shoulder to cry on. I needed someone to comfort me."

"I'm not just a shoulder for you to cry on; I'm so much more than that—we both know that."

"What we both *know* is that I'm married. And while my husband is not perfect, he is my husband and I made a pledge to him and God. I pledged my life to him."

"He doesn't deserve your life! You hardly ever see him. Although you don't talk about it with me, it's obvious he has a drug problem. It's okay if you want to renege on your pledge to him."

"No, it's not. You think I'm just supposed to give up? That's not how marriage should work. I'm not just in it as long as things are good—that ain't right. Love is hard. Relationships aren't easy. Sometimes we get things right, but a lot of the time—most of the time we don't. That doesn't mean we should give up, jump ship, and stop trying."

"So what are you saying? I was just for the moment? You want to dump me and see if you can't make your marriage work?"

"Gerald, I wouldn't exactly use those words, but I guess yes, I do want to re-focus on my marriage."

"That's insane. Darryn will never be able to shower you with the kind of love that I can."

"Gerald, we both know this is best. Think of this as a goodbye," Madetra said as she reached out to tenderly touch the side of his face.

He kissed her hands softly, tenderly. He touched her in a way that reminded her she was all woman. As she dropped her hands to her side, he dropped to his knees and nuzzled his face between her legs.

"Ohhhh . . . Gerald . . ." Before she could complete the sentence, his moist, warm tongue was on her clit. "You know what they say about break up sex!" she said laughing.

He grinned, self-assured. "Yep, I know." He spread her lips and forged his tongue deeper inside her, continuing the cat-and-mouse game between his tongue and her clit. With his mouth, he encouraged the heat of her moisture to rise and bubble up until she exploded. Wanting to return the favor, she unzipped his jeans, and quickly enveloped his manhood in the warmth of her mouth.

After nearly thirty minutes of pleasuring each other in the 69 position, they decided to take things to the next level.

"Tell me you love me, Mad," Gerald whispered in her ear as he entered her there on the floor.

She hated the whole "whose-stuff-is-this" game men always played, but she was horny, so she decided to play along. "I love you," she said half-heartedly.

She was instantly rewarded with a half-hearted thrust.

"Say it again, baby," Gerald demanded urgently.

"I love you," she told him, this time with feeling.

Again she was rewarded with a thrust that was much deeper, sending a flurry of sensations to all parts of her body. "Say that again, baby," he roughly ordered.

"I!"

Thrust.

"LOVE!"

Thrust.

"YOU!"

Thrust.

"GERALD!"

Thrust.

"Whose stuff is this?"

Madetra smiled to herself.

"Yours, baby!"

Thrust.

"Whose . . . is . . . this?"

"It's . . . yours . . . baby!"

Thrust.

"This tight, wet stuff is all mine, ain't it, baby?"

"YES."

Thrust.

"IT'S . . ."

Thrust.

"ALL . . ."

Thrust.

"YOURS . . ."

Thrust.

"GERALD!"

Thrust.

They spent the next hour playing out similar variations of the same theme, that, emotionally, they still belonged exclusively to one another despite the fact they were going to be physically apart. In the aftermath of their sin, they lay silently holding each other.

"This doesn't change anything," Madetra said.

Gerald lightly kissed her forehead.

"I know."

"I do love you, you know that too, don't you?" Madetra asked quietly.

"Yep. I heard. So does this mean I can no longer give you massages?"

"Let's play that by ear. You rubbing all over me is bound to give me wicked thoughts." They both laughed.

Within minutes, Gerald was dressed, and Madetra was walking with him naked to the door.

"If you don't mind, I'm going to pass on the day of sightseeing."

"I understand," she said. "I'm suddenly not in the mood much for it either.

They kissed each other long and passionately just outside of the door, not caring who might see them.

Unfortunately for Gerald and Madetra, someone who'd been watching them for a while was just down the hall with a camera, capturing their x-rated moment on film.

Their personal paparazzi had been patiently watching, waiting, wanting them to be sloppy and reckless like they had been in Jamaica, and now the person documenting their lustful sins was fully prepared to take advantage of Gerald's and Madetra's carelessness and mistakes.

"I don't care what you say, but this isn't goodbye," Gerald told Madetra when they came up for air.

"Gerald . . ."

"I'm not threatening you; don't get scared. I'm not going to call and harass you or anything like that. It's actually going to be you coming after me. You just wait and see. Mark my words."

They kissed again, and then he left.

Mad didn't care what Gerald said. She was never going to talk to him or see him again. There was too much at stake. She was permanently closing that chapter of her life and was looking forward to a future spent repairing her marriage.

DESTANIE

The next day, Destanie took a sip from her Long Island Iced Tea while she waited for her guest.

The person she was meeting was over twenty minutes late, but that was of no surprise to Destanie. She expected nothing less than for her guest to show her utter lack of class. Just as she was thinking of her preferred way of telling her drinking companion off, she appeared in the doorway of the hotel restaurant's bar.

"Finally," Destanie mumbled under her breath as she waved in the direction of the door.

Kay rolled her eyes and slowly walked toward Destanie.

Kaylantra was not in the mood for Desperate Destanie, but she had to admit, she couldn't pass up the chance to rub in Destanie's face the fact that she now was living with her ex-lover.

"It's about time you showed up," Destanie said with an attitude when Kay sat in the seat beside her at the bar.

"Before you start getting on my nerves, can I order me a drink?" Kay ordered an apple martini from a nearby sexy, beefy bartender, and while he mixed her drink, the two of them eyed each other the whole time.

"You're really disgusting—you'll pick up anything walking, won't you? Look, since we both can't stand each other, I'm going to cut to the chase and make this brief. I have been following you for the last couple of weeks to see what all the fuss is about. For the life of me, I still don't understand what Finney sees in you," Destanie said.

"You may want to just straight out ask him because he obviously sees something in me that he finds appealing that he didn't see in you," Kay responded, gloating.

"I would ask him, but the truth is, he doesn't really know you. Or I'm sure he doesn't know the side of you I've seen. I've been going to your little strip club in the cut. I've been checking you out on Thursday nights. It's been eye-opening."

Kay could feel the blood rush to her cheeks, but she tried to keep her composure. "I hope you've been enjoying the shows," she said as she gulped down her drink.

"It's not my thang, you know—with your stretch marks, cellulite, sagging breasts and all."

"You must have me confused with your damn self . . . 'cause ain't none of that stuff you mentioned located anywhere on this body."

"Like I said, you're not my type, but I noticed a lot of other people did enjoy your shows. There was one man in particular. It would seem you have a very special friend who not only enjoys your shows, but he really enjoys your company. From what I've seen, the two of you like to play dirty games. He likes to keep you in the dark. It would seem he likes to be in total control."

"What are you talking about?" Kay asked, hoping she didn't reek of fear.

"I know what your little or, should I say, big friend looks like. Which is more than you can say. I got pictures. Wanna see him?"

"You're crazy, and I'm not interested in anything you have to show me." Kay stood up to leave.

"Hmmm . . . well, maybe Finney would be interested in seeing them, or better yet, maybe your sister."

"What has my sister or Finesse got to do with anything?"

"I don't know; you tell me." Destanie handed Kay some 8 ½ X 11 glossy color photos.

What Kay saw stopped her cold. She fell back into her chair in disbelief. Staring her in the face were pictures of her blindfolded and having sex with Darryn—the brother-in-law she hated! "What is this? Is it some kind of sick joke? How did you doctor these up? Why did you doctor these up? Are you that desperate to win Finney back?"

"Oh, so you're using the R. Kelly defense? That ain't you, right? It's someone that looks like you! Whatever! You know and I know that nothing has been doctored up. You really are as dumb as you look. It seems you and your $1,000-a-night customer like to get your freak on. And for just a little bit of cash under the table your pimp, I mean boss, Eddie, let me take these real candid shots."

"You're crazy! How could Darryn do this? Why would he do this?"

"Obviously, someone has a crush on you. I never

bought that 'smoldering-hatred' act you and him have been playing. The real question is, how could you do what you did? Why would you have sex, albeit protected sex, with a stranger—sight unseen? Money makes you do funny and nasty things, huh?"

Kay couldn't answer her. Since things had gotten serious between her and Finney, she'd meant to stop having sex with her patron, but the money had been too good to turn down.

Since she'd always been careful to use protection, she figured a few more weeks wouldn't have mattered. In a few more weeks, she had planned to look for a legit job.

Tears of remorse gathered in her eyes and fell like hot coals down her cheeks. She stared at the pictures in front of her.

Had she stopped, there would be no pictures of her having sex with her brother-in-law. There would be no evidence of her deep betrayal of her sister, the one person in her life who truly loved her unconditionally and always had her back.

"I bet that's how all your men like you, huh? Speechless. Sluts are like kids; they should be seen and not heard. And speaking of kids—you're going to have one for me."

"What? What did you say?"

"You heard me. If you don't want your sister and Finney to see these pictures, you're going to be a surrogate mother for me. And if you refuse, in the words of Ricky Ricardo, 'you're gonna have some 'splaining to do," Destanie said with a laugh.

"You're even crazier than I thought. You have lost your mind if you think I'm going to ruin my body and give up an innocent baby to your crazy

ass! Man, where's the crack you've been smoking?"
Kay asked.

"Let me be real clear. Because of Finney, I had
an abortion and now because of an infection, endometriosis and excess scar tissue, I can't have
kids. I think it's only fitting that his precious girlfriend helps me fix my childless situation. Plus,
with your body destroyed by stretch marks and a
baby pouch and maybe some excess weight you
can't get rid of, I'm sure it will only be a matter of
time before Finney's caught-up-on-looks ass is searching for someone else, and he won't have far to look."

"You have lost your mind. You're doing all this
to win Finney back?"

"Everything I do is because of him. Just look at
it this way—if you don't agree to my plan, I will
ruin your sister and her marriage; plus, I'll reveal
to Finesse what a slut you really are. Once he sees
these pictures, he'll dump you so fast, your head
will swim."

"How am I going to explain being pregnant all
of a sudden?"

"That's your problem. Tell him that you're
doing it out of the kindness of your heart to make
up for him having me kill our baby! I don't care.
All I know is you have twenty-four hours to get
back with me regarding your decision. I want an
answer by the time we leave Vegas."

"I don't need twenty-four hours. I'm telling you
HELL-TO-THE-NAW right now," Kay said defiantly.

"You're a simple, selfish, triflin' somethin'. Like
I said before, what my former flame sees in you is
beyond me—oh, that's right—you're a slut—a freaking whore-prostitute who is screwing her sister's

husband for money. And you were so dumb, you didn't even know."

The thought of having sex with her sister's husband, a man she couldn't stand, made Kay ill. "I should jack you up right now for bringing this mess to me."

"Please . . . you brought it on yourself. We can go there right now if you want to, but it's not going to change the fact that you're one stupid bit—"

Before the sentence was fully out of her mouth, Kay backhanded Destanie and knocked her to the floor.

Filled with the fury of a cyclone, Destanie jumped up from the floor in full-force attack mode. She grabbed what was remaining in her glass and threw the liquid on Kay and then lunged forward, grabbing for Kay's neck.

The diners in the restaurant couldn't believe their eyes as Kay and Destanie tumbled around on the ground for what seemed like forever. As the two women pulled each other's hair and kicked and slapped at each other, a male diner and the bartender who had fixed Kay's drink pulled them apart.

"I've changed my mind. You have twelve hours. If I don't hear from you by nine in the morning, you can kiss your world as you know it goodbye," Destanie informed Kay as she fought to release herself from the diner's grasp. "And by the way, I'll get you a set of the pictures. They're time and date stamped. Won't Finney find that interesting?"

"Shut the hell up," Kay yelled before grabbing her purse and storming out of the restaurant.

Oblivious to the fact that she looked like Tina Turner following her Vegas fight with Ike in the limo,

Kay ran through the lobby and toward the hotel exit as people pointed and stared.

Kay had never in her life wanted kids, and the thought of having one as a surrogate for the craziest woman she knew was not her idea of a good time. Just the thought of getting pregnant nauseated her—she tossed her cookies just as Finesse appeared in front of her in the lobby.

He looked in disbelief as she vomited all over his designer pants and shoes. "Babe, you okay?" he asked.

"What do you think? Do I look okay? I just threw up all over you—that's a sure sign that I'm NOT okay."

"Okay, breathe, babe," he told her while rubbing her back.

"D-don't y-you t-tell m-me t-to b-breathe," Kay said, unable to catch her breath. "You and your stupid ex and her stupid obsession with you, you've both made my life miserable. You're the reason I'm in the mess I'm in now," Kay said before sprinting from the scene like a track star running toward some unseen finish line.

"Kay! Wait! Wait! What's up? What are you talking about?" Finesse yelled after her.

Kay ran as far as her legs would take her, and when she couldn't run anymore, she got into a cab and rode around the city for hours. While she had technically won the fight with Destanie, she eventually started to feel the pain from the scratches, kicks, and hits Destanie managed to get in.

Destanie's child? As Kay thought about her situation, she toyed for a few moments with the idea of going to Madetra and Finney with the truth, but after thinking about it for a while, she knew she really had no choice. She had to do what she was being asked to do—no, being blackmailed into doing.

Kay knew that if she didn't do what Destanie wanted, two people she loved would be destroyed, and she just couldn't let that happen. Kay knew what she had to do and she knew that the next nine months of her life would be pure hell.

"Stripped of your ordinary surroundings, you are forced into direct experience. Such direct experience inevitably makes you aware of who it is that is having the experience. That's not always comfortable, but it is always invigorating."
~ Michael Crichton

FINESSE

Finesse had no idea why Kaylantra was so upset when he saw her, but based on what little she had said, it was obvious that Destanie had something to do with it. His radar went off when he saw Destanie in the hotel lobby, trailing just minutes behind Kay.

Destanie looked just as bad, if not worse than Kay. It was obvious the two of them had been in a fight. Finesse knew he was likely the source of the brawl and was determined to find out what and who started it. Finesse was done with Destanie and had been for a long time. She knew that he was serious about Kaylantra, so he couldn't understand why she was still trying so hard to hold on to something that had been dead a long while.

Determined for once and for all to let Destanie know where he stood, Finesse grabbed her by the arm as she passed him in the lobby. "We need to talk," he said gruffly. He guided her down a long, narrow, secluded hallway, past water fountains and restrooms, and then pushed her into a large, over-sized phone booth.

"What do you think you're doing?" Destanie asked, secretly thrilled to be stuck alone with him in such tight quarters.

"What just happened between you and Kay?"

"Why don't you ask her?"

"Hello—I did; she wouldn't tell me, so that's why I'm asking you."

"What if I said there was nothing to tell?"

"I'd say you were lying. You both look like you were in a boxing match, and I'm wearing her vomit, for some reason. So I know something went down and the quicker you tell me what went down between you two, the quicker I'll be able to get out of here and take off these funky clothes."

"I can help you get out of your clothes right now, if you want," Destanie suggested seductively while tugging at his belt.

"Destanie, keep your hands off me, and tell me what happened with Kay!"

"Fine. You want to know what happened? Your crazy girlfriend attacked me. The next time she does that, I'm going to have her arrested for assault."

"Hmmm. Why do I think you had something to do with provoking her?"

"You always think the worst of me—why is that, Finney? You haven't always been that way."

"Destanie, you have to stop living in the past. You sweat me at work. I had to change both my cell and home phone numbers because of your damn stupid messages. I've moved on; you should too. I don't know what your beef was about with Kay, but she's my present . . . my future. You're my past . . . my never-gonna-be."

"I could make you so happy, if only you'd give me the chance."

The combination of the stench from his clothes, the lack of oxygen in the phone booth, and the close proximity of Destanie's soft, bodacious curves intoxicated Finney and made him lightheaded.

Sensing that Finesse wasn't as in control as he wanted to be, Destanie went in for the kill. She purposely dropped her purse and bent over to collect its contents, knowing full well she was wearing the skimpiest of thongs. She rested her palms on the phone booth's small bench and used it for support. Then, with her backside totally exposed, she backed up and grinded her pelvis into Finney's hardening member.

Nearly giving in to the dog in him, Finesse caught himself just in time and backed away from Destanie's tempting, upturned ass. "What are you doing, Destanie? Don't disrespect yourself or what we had like that! Come on, get up!" he said, his voice oozing compassion. "Let's just forget that we were ever here! Kay will tell me what happened between the two of you in her own time when she is good and ready!" He left Destanie feeling discouraged, embarrassed and crying her eyes out in the phone booth.

Well, that didn't exactly work out very well, Finesse thought to himself as he walked through the hotel's lobby, trying hard to hide the ever-growing wood in his pants.

DARRYN

Driving through the grittier, industrial side of Vegas, Darryn, The Trash Man, was forced to finally come to terms with the fact that he was a drug addict who was likely never going to get over his habit. As he drove down unfamiliar, narrow streets littered with trash and junk cars, he couldn't help wondering how this all happened.

His ass-toe was twitching. That meant trouble.

He absentmindedly parked his rental car and shooed away a scantily dressed white hooker in her twenties who approached him. He had a purpose. He was on a mission. He had never before robbed anyone, but he needed either some rock or some money. He got out of the car, grabbed a nearby broken bottle from the ground and hid in an alley beside a small, out-of-the-way bank on the south side of town.

After just a few moments, a decently dressed white man walked past him with a bank deposit bag in his hands. Darryn sized him up. He guessed the man wasn't rolling in dough, but had more money than he did. From the looks of him, Darryn presumed the man owned his own company somewhere in the area.

Darryn steeled his nerves and prepared to rob the man. With broken bottle in hand, he rushed his victim from behind. The two men scuffled until Darryn eventually got the upper hand. "I ain't trying to hurt nobody!" Darryn yelled. "I just need a little money! I just need a few dollars!"

"I don't have any money on me!" the frightened man yelled back. "There are mostly checks in this bag!"

"I ain't trying to hear that mess! Give me the bag and your wallet!"

"I'm not giving you this bag and my wallet!"

"Hand over that bag and your wallet or your ass is gonna wind up full of glass!"

His victim hesitated, unsure of what to do. That made two of them. Darryn no longer recognized himself. He had never stolen anything in his life from anyone, not even from his parents, which was considered a rite of passage for most teens. The idea of threatening somebody's life for a few dollars sickened him.

"Why don't you put down that bottle and go down the street to the shelter?" the scared man in front of Darryn asked while trying to bargain for his money and his life.

Darryn started laughing. He was willing to play along. "I did go down to the shelter, and there ain't no more room."

The man reached into the bag and counted out some money. "I don't believe you. Here, I'll give you fifty bucks, if you promise me you'll go right down the street there to the shelter. They can help you clean yourself up. They can help you get off of drugs and booze. I know; I donate money to them every year."

Darryn laughed some more. This was one of the most inane conversations he'd ever had in his life.

"Look, I'll tell you what . . . here's my card . . . take the fifty bucks and go get yourself cleaned up and then give me a call. That number is my cell phone number. I may just have a job for you once you get yourself together."

The man tried to hand Darryn his card and some money, but instead of taking it, Darryn burst into laughter. "Look, I'll tell *you* what . . . this is how it's gonna go down. You are going to give me all of the money in your deposit bag and in your wallet, and then the two of us are going to walk away in opposite directions and pretend like this never happened." He stretched out his arm and locked eyes with the man in front of him.

"No can do, man. Give a man a fish and he eats once; teach him to fish and he eats for a lifetime. God can only help those willing to help themselves. Meet me halfway, partner."

"Are you kidding me?" Darryn asked, his patience running thin. "I will kill you if you don't give me all your fucking money and stop talking about fish!"

The shelter donor once again tried to hand Darryn his card.

Frustrated, Darryn lunged at the man, and he fell to the ground. To Darryn's surprise, the man lay on the ground motionless with the broken bottle jutting out of his chest.

Darryn stared without blinking at the man in

front of him as blood gushed from his body. The sanguine, life-sustaining liquid that had previously traveled through his veins was now quickly covering the sidewalk, as if trying desperately to escape the ghastly prison that had been his body.

Darryn felt some presence other than his own pry the deposit bag out of the man's hands. He opened the bag and quickly noted it contained three thousand dollars, which he stuffed in his pockets. He then searched the man's lifeless body for his wallet, where he located another two hundred dollars. Darryn flipped through the wallet and looked briefly at pictures and the man's ID—Preston.

The man he killed was named Preston Marks. In that moment, Darryn promised himself that he would never think about Preston Marks again.

Darryn drove directly back to the hotel after his encounter with Preston. He'd never before watched anyone die so violently, and it was a vision he desperately wanted to get out of his mind. His plan to do just that was uncomplicated and pretty straight forward. He was going to go back to the hotel, where he'd clean himself up. Next, he was going to go out and buy himself some blow on The Strip and then he was going to snort himself senseless.

His plan was simple enough. Unfortunately, he hadn't planned on his big-mouth sister-in-law greeting him in the hotel lobby.

"A journey of a thousand miles must begin with a single step."
~ Lao Tzu

KAYLANTRA

"What the hell is wrong with you?" Kay asked right before she slapped Darryn hard across his face once she saw him enter the hotel.

His face immediately stung, and blood rushed to the site where he'd been tagged. "What's wrong with you? Why the hell did you just slap me?"

"I just saw some pictures that kind of surprised me."

"And I care because . . . ?"

"Because your ass was in the pictures screwing me!"

"Kay, what are you talking about?"

"What are you usually doing on Thursday nights, Darryn?"

A cocksure smirk crept across his face that angered her, and she raised her arm to slap him once more.

He grabbed it in mid-air. "Don't slap me again."

Knowing that he was every bit as crazy as she was, Kay heeded his warning. "Is there some particular reason you felt the need to screw me while being married to my sister?"

"Isn't the reason obvious? Look at you—who wouldn't want you? Did the thought ever occur to you that, over the years, I've fallen in love with you?"

"I thought you hated me! I sure as hell hate you! You buster! We argue with each other every chance we get! I look just like my sister; I'm a duplicate of something you already have, you idiot!"

"No, you're not! Believe me. You're what Madetra used to be, and for the record, I only argue with you all the time because it's a way of getting your attention."

"You are sick and out of your damn mind!"

"And you are easy. You shouldn't have been so desperate for money and so quick to screw a stranger!"

"I know you're not trying to justify your dirt, you friggin' cokehead!"

"At least I kept my head all in the family. I'm not ashamed of what I've done!"

"How can you say that? You should be! You had sex with me for nearly a year while you were married to my sister—how can you not be ashamed?"

"I know you ain't trying to stand there and be the moral police, judging me! Let's recap your life, shall we? What exactly do you do for a living? That's right, you shake your behind for money and charge strange men to watch you have orgasms on the Internet. And by the way, in case you didn't know I'm SoulViewer—Elvis dust or bust, baby!"

It couldn't be! Over the past year, she and Soul-Viewer had gotten close. How could he possibly be the same man that she hated so much?

"So how did you find out I was your special

Thursday-night friend?" Darryn asked, oblivious to the fact that his news about SoulViewer had devastated her.

"Does it matter?"

"No, not really. Does Finney know? Does Madetra?"

"No, not yet, no," Kay said, stumbling over her words.

"Good, and Mad better not ever find out; it's all water under the bridge. I heard through the grapevine you were giving up that life. My loss. Oh well . . . life goes on." Darryn winked at her and walked toward the elevators.

"You're right, Darryn," Kay said as she watched him walk away, "life does go on."

*   *   *   *   *   *   *

"Kay! Darryn!" Madetra yelled.

Not ready to face her sister, Kay started to walk through the lobby as if she didn't hear her.

Madetra quickly caught up with her. "What is this I've heard about a fight between you and Destanie? I saw Finney not too long ago."

"I don't want to talk about it, Mad."

"Spill it!" Madetra ordered, stopping Kay in her tracks.

"Okay! You want to know what's going on? Destanie just informed me that she wants me to carry a child for her as a surrogate."

"What? Is she crazy?"

"Nope. Actually she has my ass over a barrel—she has pictures of me having sex with a client. The pictures are time and date stamped, and if Finney sees them, he'll know I've been sleeping around on him."

"You're kidding me. You're not giving in to her blackmail scheme, are you?"

"Yep. She thinks that if I have a baby, Finesse will find my body totally repulsive and leave me. She mistakenly thinks he'll go running back to her."

"So how are you gonna explain just being pregnant all of a sudden to him?"

"I'm giving up my selfish ways and choosing to do something for someone else out of the kindness of my heart."

"That's comical."

"What?—the kindness of my heart part?"

"Finney won't buy that for a second. You can't be serious about actually doing this, Kay."

"What choice do I have? Look, I have to go. I'll see you later," Kay said sadly before running away.

MADETRA

One rainy Saturday a few weeks later, Madetra's ringing cell phone woke her up from a deep sleep. She'd been back for weeks but was still trying to catch up for her lack of sleep in Las Vegas. "Yeah?" she muttered, as if daring someone to be calling her with a medical emergency.

"Oh, what a tangled web we weave, when first we practice to deceive. A spouse that cheats deserves no mercy. That is why sexually, you'll serve me. Blackmail ain't a pretty game, but then again neither is shame. Gotcha! Meet me at McCormick & Schmick's for lunch. Be there at twelve noon. Don't be late," a gruff, obviously disguised voice, whispered into the phone before hanging up.

Stunned, Madetra willed herself to call a number that she was surprised she even remembered. "I got your message, Gerald! You don't have to call with silly, obscene messages. If you want me, just say you do, and stop playing games . . . not that you could ever have me permanently. You wouldn't know what to do with me if you did get me."

"Madetra . . ." Gerald started.

"For the record, you were just something for me to do in Jamaica and Vegas. You were just for the moment. I'm married. I need to focus on my husband and our marriage. So you can waste your time trying to blackmail me if you want. Who do you think my husband will believe? I think he'll believe me over a loser like you . . ."

As she was speaking, Gerald St. John threw his cell phone against the farthest wall in his apartment, shattering it into a million pieces.

"Hello? Hello?" Madetra yelled into the phone before hanging up good and pissed.

What happens in Vegas, stays in Vegas, my behind, she thought.

Las Vegas had been her downfall. Talk about your bad ideas. DAT Club was a mistake from day one. After all of their trips, tons of drama had taken place in the lives of the people she cared about. She and her husband were more estranged than ever; her sister was planning on having a baby for a crazy woman she couldn't stand; and she herself had risked her marriage and career for a little extra piece on the side.

She was officially living a nightmare. But what was done was done. Now it was time to pay the price. While her early gut feelings told her the blackmailer was probably Gerald, the more she thought about it, the less she believed it. Gerald was harmless, a sweetheart and at one time he truly loved her. He only wanted what was best for her.

As she thought more about it, Madetra was sure

that Gerald wasn't the one blackmailing her about her dirty deeds. Apparently someone else knew what they had been up to, and she hoped that that person wouldn't spill the beans to her husband. She took comfort in the fact that in a few short hours she would know who the tormentor of her soul was and she was comforted even more by the fact that her blackmailer would soon know what the wrath of a calculating woman felt like.

*   *   *   *   *   *   *

As she walked toward her blackmailer in the restaurant at straight up noon, Madetra had to keep herself from laughing. "You're my big, bad threat? My, my, E'an, what a busy boy you've been," she said as she slipped into the seat across from him. "And here I was thinking you'd turned over a new leaf."

"A man has to do something to keep you on your toes," he said with a slow smile. "Although I have to admit, my feelings are a bit hurt. I've been pursuing you all year, and you've done nothing but reject me. Yet then you open your legs for the first little drug dealer that comes along. I'm a little pissed that you've had an affair with someone that wasn't me."

Madetra laughed. "So you intend on blackmailing me for sex? My, you're desperate."

"The way I see it, if you don't want your husband to know you've been wrapping that tight, beautiful body of yours around that loser baseball-playing wannabe, you're going to have to wrap it around me."

"You're crazier than your patients."

"That is true . . . most days."

"So how did you find out about me and Gerald? When did you find out? Did you find out in Jamaica or Vegas?"

"It doesn't matter, as long as I get what I want. And if it makes a difference, I have pictures," he said with a wink.

"What? Are you kidding me? You're serious? You're really planning on blackmailing me into having sex with you?"

"Yep, what I saw in Jamaica and Vegas would not make your man very happy. After all, you were blowing another man and standing in a hallway naked while kissing another man . . . the man that sells your husband crack, if I'm not mistaken. Or didn't you know that?"

Hatred filled Madetra's eyes as she stared him down. She couldn't believe that the man she'd been sleeping with on the side was undermining her marriage by supplying drugs to her husband.

"You're a spiteful bastard! Okay, fine, I'll have meaningless, awful sex with you. How do you think you'll like being second best, second banana, second fiddle? Because when I leave you, just remember I'll be going home to the man I really love, the man I really want to screw."

"Who? The crackhead?" E'an laughed. "Yeah. I'm real jealous of your husband, the drug addict." E'an wasn't letting Madetra Price into his head. She could just drop the bull with him. Most proud men hated the idea of sharing what was theirs with others. "I'll like being second best just fine. Here's the deal—we'll be getting together at least once a week, every Thursday for sex, at my discretion; it may be more than once a week, so stay flexible."

"Are you kidding me?" Madetra asked incredulously.

"I'll call you on your cell every Thursday morning before you leave home for work to let you know what I have planned for us. Keep in mind I'm going to take great pleasure in making you squirm, so things are going to get demented and twisted. Lots of sex in public, lots of painful sex aids, that kind of thing. With each passing week, I'm going to enjoy doing increasingly demeaning and naughty things to you."

"You're going to get yours one day, E'an Shaw."

"That may be, but it won't happen until after I get yours—over and over and over again."

Her words meant very little to him. She didn't realize it, but she had long ago filled him with a low simmering rage that made him secretly hate her, and now that he had the chance, nothing would deter him from his path to destroy her.

Two weeks later, Madetra's nightmare began.

* * * * * * *

She got an early Thursday morning phone call telling her she was to meet E'an at her husband's place of business at five on the dot wearing nothing but a raincoat and 5-inch high stilettos. The implication was obvious—they'd start their unholy alliance by having sex right under her husband's nose.

She'd mentioned to someone in the office that her husband worked late now every night, and E'an was taking full advantage of that knowledge. After a long day at the clinic, Madetra arrived at her husband's accounting office not knowing what to expect.

E'an was already standing in front of the building. Upon seeing her, he insisted she use her copy of her husband's key to get them in the building. E'an made it clear that he was planning on having sex with her in the office next to her husband's, calmly explaining that she would be exposed as an adulteress that very night, if she refused.

Once they slipped into the building and got on the elevator that would take them to her husband's floor, Madetra was filled with dread as she remembered security cameras were everywhere. "I can't do this!" she whispered as the elevator arrived at its destination.

"What choice do you have? Which way to your husband's office?"

She led him through a set of ornate glass doors and down a long hallway. Her husband's deep booming voice talking on the phone could be heard the farther down the hallway they walked.

"In here," her hated Lothario ordered. He pulled her into the office next to the one belonging to her husband. Upon entering the room, E'an Shaw's hands immediately started unbuttoning her clothing. He peeled her out of her raincoat in record time. His hands on her soft body turned her stomach.

"Let me get a good look at you at your fine body. Turn around, slowly," E'an instructed. Madetra did as she was told, cringing and hating every agonizing moment.

"Man, you look hot wearing nothing but that sultry-ass look and heels."

"You're mistaking sultry for hatred."

"Like that matters. Turn around again," he ordered.

Madetra fumed but obeyed. She had half a mind to go over to her husband's office and confess her affair herself—consequences be damned. Anything would be better than the torture she was going through.

"Keep turning . . ."

"E'an you can kiss . . .

Before she could finish, he had slid on a condom, pushed her forcefully onto the room's large desk, pried her legs open with his thighs, and violently lodged himself inside of her without the benefit of foreplay. As office supplies poked her in the butt and back and E'an poked in and out of her dryness, she winced. "You are beyond sick and twisted," Madetra said, spitting venom.

Her contempt was met with a sadistic smile. *He was extremely turned on by her immense displeasure and disgust.* What he once hated—her out and out disdain for him—now fueled his passion. Her increasingly dismissive attitude only made him want to degrade and humiliate her more. The more Madetra made him feel like less than a man, the more overbearingly manly he became.

When Madetra heard her husband hang up the phone, she sharply inhaled. At first, the muffled sounds and whispering startled Darryn—that is until he realized what was going on in the room next door. It was always the quiet, shy, and unassuming ones that turned out to be freaks. He'd been working in the office beside Pamela Cole for years but had no idea that she liked to get busy after hours in her office.

Darryn listened for a while to the staccato breathing coming from the other side of his office wall. *The poor woman sounded like she was in pain.* Curiosity about what his fine office mate looked like naked got the best of him. Like most of the men in the office, he'd fantasized about her.

Before his curiosity killed him, he got up from his seat, moved stealthily around his desk, opened his door, and entered the hallway. Just as he was about to crack open the door to his co-worker's office, his phone rang. Hoping it would be his wife receptive to the idea of phone sex, he turned on his heels and hurried back into his office.

Not knowing how close she came to being discovered by her husband, Madetra prayed for E'an to die as he pummeled and pounded her nether region incessantly.

That was only the beginning.

For the next several months, E'an virtually tormented Madetra. Occasionally, he felt sorry for her. He'd often want nothing more than to take her in his arms and hold her. He wanted to tell her that in truth he actually cared for her. He wanted to wipe her tears away and erase her pain, but then, his memory of those years of rejection would resurface to remind him of his purpose.

His favorite humiliation of Madetra occurred when he drove with her during morning rush-hour traffic to the exit ramp that her husband used on his way to work. He'd park the car on the shoulder of the road, and no matter what sexual position they used, he'd make sure the beautiful face that haunted his dreams was always facing the window.

All it would take for Darryn to see his wife with

another man would be for him to take an extended look out of his car's passenger window.

E'an prayed for the day when that would happen, and Madetra prayed equally as hard for that day to never come.

"I think that wherever your journey takes you, there are new gods waiting there, with divine patience—and laughter."
~ Susan M. Watkins

KAYLANTRA

Kay moved in with Finesse after they returned from Jamaica, and they'd been blissfully playing house ever since. She knew she had to tell him about the decision she'd made since their trip to Vegas, but since she didn't know how best to say it, she just spat it out.

As they sat together watching pro basketball on his Plasma TV one rainy Sunday afternoon, she announced, "I just thought you should know, Finney—I've decided to be a surrogate for Destanie."

"That's cool, babe," he said without looking up from the game. It took another full ten seconds for Kay's words to sink in, and when they did, his reaction was a helluva lot different. "You're going to do what?" he exploded.

Knowing that this wouldn't be an easy conversation, Kay jumped in with attitude to spare. "You heard me—I'm going to act as a surrogate for your old girlfriend and give her the one thing she wants more than anything—a baby! That would keep her busy and off our backs, wouldn't it?" she asked with a fake smile.

"Have you lost your mind? Why would you want to carry a baby for her?"

"Look, she and I had a heart-to-heart on our last trip, and I thought this was the least I could do."

"Heart-to-heart, my ass. Stop being sarcastic. You two got into a fight! And for the record, the least you can do is not a doggone thing! What am I missing? Why do you want to carry a child for Destanie, of all people?"

"I feel guilty because you made her have an abortion, and now she can't have kids. Like I said, it's the least I could do."

"Don't lay that mess on me. That's between the two of us. I didn't make her have an abortion; I merely suggested that she have one. What she did has nothing to do with you. You don't owe her a thing, and neither do I. We're all responsible ultimately for our own actions, and she needs to deal with what she's done on her own. I'm at peace with what I did, and I don't need you trying to make up for anything I did or didn't do."

"Look at you—you're sounding pretty selfish to me."

"It's got nothing to do with being selfish. What you're talking about doing isn't normal. I thought you hated her. How are you going to carry a child for nine months and grow attached to it, just to give it up to a woman you can't stand? A woman that is out of her fucking mind, I might add! That would be emotionally hard for you—no, make that emotionally impossible for you."

"I can handle it."

"No, you can't. You're strong and all, but why

deal with any unnecessary mess? Need I remind you that the two of you were boxing not too long ago? You hate her, remember?"

"When she and I got together in Vegas, it was our come-to-Jesus meeting."

"You can shut that down; it was more like a come-to-crazy meeting. From the way you both looked after the 'meeting' it seemed like y'all tried to kill each other. I can't allow you to carry a baby and then give it away to that crazy, unfit nut, Kay."

Kay looked at him and laughed. "You can't allow me to decide what to do with my body? Are you kidding me? Did you really form your mouth to say that? I know you don't think you can tell me what to do with my body!" she yelled in mock defiance.

"Hold up! None of this makes sense. What's really going on, babe?"

"I thought I would try something new. For once in my life, I'm trying to not think of myself. I'm trying not to be selfish, and it would be nice if my man could support me," she said as she tried to cuddle with him on the sofa.

He brushed her off. "I can't support you on this, Kay! It just doesn't make sense. Before you delivered a baby for Destanie, you'd kill each other. So are you going to tell her you won't be having a baby for her, or do I need to tell her?" Finesse asked in a cocky tone. His smug belief that they actually controlled their own fates and destinies had Kay almost believing it too.

She sighed deeply. "It's too late," she said, fighting back tears. "I'm already pregnant. I was implanted a few months ago with an embryo made up of her egg and some random guy's sperm."

"I can't believe you would do something like this without talking to me first. You have lost your damn mind! You are not keeping this baby!"

"Stop telling me what I can and can't do with my body!"

"You're as crazy as Destanie! I feel sorry for the poor child you're carrying!" he yelled as he grabbed his jacket and left.

As she listened to his car back out of the drive, Kay knew her world was about to be very different, but she had no idea just how unrecognizable it would become.

DESTANIE

Embarrassing and humiliating her ex-boyfriend's current girlfriend gave Destanie a tremendous amount of pleasure, and the day they met for lunch at Gates Bar-B-Q was no different.

"So, Kay, what do you think about this nursery arrangement? Or what about this one?" Destanie asked over lunch a few days after Kay and Finney had their argument.

Kay observed Destanie and the magazine pictures gloomily. "Why do you care so much about what I think?"

"You're my baby's birth mother; you're entitled to an opinion on our child's living environment."

"I know you don't think we're going to bond during this twisted, jacked-up experience, do you? This is nothing but business, so don't you worry about my doggone opinion."

"Kay, stop being so negative. It will affect the baby. We all need to just try to make the best of an awkward situation."

An awkward situation? Kay wanted to slap Destanie. Too bad she didn't have the strength. She was exhausted. Payback was a mutha.

Over the years, she'd kicked beaucoup behind—Destanie's included—and now her baby was paying her back and kicking hers. Carrying a child had her tired all the time.

Kay absent-mindedly rubbed her tummy. Every time she thought about the tiny, little boy or girl growing inside of her, she got almost giddy. The idea that she would one day soon give life still amazed her.

"Why are you rubbing your tummy? Can you feel the baby moving?" Destanie asked while reaching over the table to touch Kay's stomach.

Kay's demeanor stopped her cold. "Touch my stomach and you die."

"There is no need to be so doggone rude."

"I'm not playing with you—touch my stomach, and I'll slap the hell out of you."

Despite the fair warning, Destanie reached over and patted Kay's belly.

As if by reflex, Kay raised her hand, and with all the force she had in her body, slapped Destanie across the face and knocked her out of her chair.

All eyes in the restaurant rested on the two of them as Destanie rushed to get up and return to her seat.

"I'm going to write that off as you being hormonal," Destanie said as she rubbed her sore jaw. "But let's get one thing straight—if you ever lay a hand on me again, the whole world will know what you've been doing with your brother-in-law."

Kay raised her hand to slap her again, but Destanie caught her by the wrist. "I would suggest you not test me. Now, are you ready to make some decisions about the nursery? Oh, instead of that, why don't we talk a little bit about your pregnancy," Destanie said in a super-sweet voice.

"Whatever," Kay said as she snatched her arm out of Destanie's grip. "I suppose you want me to do something like keep a stupid journal. That ain't ever gonna happen."

"I would never want you to do anything during the pregnancy that you weren't comfortable doing. I just wanted to let you in on a little secret; call it one of my many surprises."

"Oh goodie, why don't we just throw a surprise party?" Kay deadpanned with fake enthusiasm, dreading the bomb that Destanie would drop on her this time.

"Just in case you or Finesse try to kill my baby, you might like to know that the father is actually Finesse."

Kay couldn't believe she'd heard Destanie right. She wouldn't allow herself to believe for a minute that Finesse was the father of the baby she was carrying. "What? Don't make me kill you today, Crazy!"

"This has nothing to do with me being crazy. I'm serious. The last time we were together, I kept a little piece of him. After we made love, I kept his sperm in the condom. I rushed it down to the Cryobank, and I've had it stored there ever since. Ask him—as he was leaving I told him I had to hurry up and get to the bank. He thought I was talking about a monetary bank, but I was talking about my neighborhood sperm bank."

"But—"

"Don't get it twisted—there are no victims here; there's just a slut and a dog who never think of anyone but themselves. What we're simply dealing with are two people being forced to face the consequences of their scandalous actions."

"No, what we have here is some crazy chick that is carrying out some twisted, vindictive revenge. You're trying to tie yourself to Finesse for life."

"Hmmm . . . he's not the prize you think he is."

"Oh really? So that's why you stole his sperm and want to have his baby? That's why you're trying so hard to win him back? Because he's no big prize?"

"I wouldn't expect you to understand," Destanie said.

"Good . . . 'cause I couldn't understand this in a hundred years, no matter how hard I tried. I really don't understand why you're doing all of this. Why would you want the baby of a man who can't stand you, and why would you go through such extremes?"

"Who knows why we do what we do? The fact is I did it. I had you impregnated with my egg and his sperm. I just thought you should know that in case you ever have any thoughts of hurting this child. We're going to have such a pretty, baby, Finesse and I. You just wait and see. Oh, by the way, here is the set of pictures I promised you."

"You're sicker than I thought. I would never hurt this child, whether or not it was Finney's," Kay said, feeling her blood pressure rise. "And for you to even think like that clearly shows you're unfit."

For the second time in several months, Kay was left speechless by Destanie and before she knew what was happening, her world started spinning and she was soon laid out cold on the floor.

"Let your mind start a journey through a strange new world.
Leave all thoughts of the world you knew before.
Let your soul take you where you long to be.
Close your eyes, let your spirit start to soar and you'll live as you've never lived before."
~ Erich Fromm

KAYLANTRA

When she came to, Kay was lying in a Shawnee Mission Medical Center bed, with Finesse sitting beside her and Madetra standing over her. Both of them looked worried.

"Do you want to tell us why you passed out in the restaurant, Kay?" Mad asked, more like a sister than a doctor.

"I was with Destanie and—"

"That explains everything," Finesse exploded. "Kay, why are you doing this? The stress of carrying that baby of hers is wearing you out."

She wanted to explain that the baby was Destanie's and his but she couldn't; so instead, she turned on him. "No, you're what's wearing me out. I'm sick and tired of trying to justify myself and explain things to you! I'm tired of your stupid questions, I'm tired of you questioning my judgment about what I'm doing with my body, I'm just tired of you, period, so get out! Get out of here! Now! Just go!"

"Babe—"

"I said get out!" Kay screamed at the top of her lungs.

"Finney, you've got to go. Kay's blood pressure is already a little high, and that's not good for her or the baby," Madetra told him.

"Fine! I'm out!" he yelled as he stormed out of the hospital emergency room.

"I take it he doesn't like the idea of you carrying Desperate Destanie's baby," Madetra said, once Finney was out of hearing range.

"That's an understatement. He's not a fan of the idea," Kay responded glumly.

"Wanna talk about it?"

"Nope."

"Okay, fine. I got another question for you."

"And what do you want to bet I won't answer that one either?"

"Why are you doing this? I agree with him—this surrogate thing is a mistake."

"Mad, you know I have no choice. Am I going to have to kick you out of here too? I don't want to talk about Destanie, me, Finesse, or the baby."

"Okay, fine! And to answer your question—no, you don't have to kick me out! I know when I'm not welcome, when my company isn't wanted. I know when it's time to go—on my own. For the record, you're fine. I'll go ahead and discharge you, and you can leave whenever you want."

Left alone with her thoughts, Kay burst into tears. How could she admit to Finesse and her sister the sordid, dirty deeds she had unknowingly carried out with Mad's husband?

When she had no more tears to cry, Kay got out of the hospital bed and slowly walked to the hospital's main entryway. The sky was overrun with dark and heavy clouds, and rain was falling in sheets by the time she made it outside. Once she exited the hospital, she immediately locked eyes with Finesse, who was sitting near the exit in the SUV her sister helped her buy.

She walked over to him, determined to tell him the truth—at least partially. "I'm sorry," she said quietly as she climbed into the seat beside him. "I'm not upset with you, I'm really mad at myself. I couldn't bring myself to tell you something really important. It's something that you really need to know."

"Kay, don't you know you can tell me anything?"

"This is our baby," she said simply. She dared time to move as she waited for him to respond. "I'm carrying our baby. And I've decided I'm not giving him or her up to that conniving, Desperate Destanie!"

"What are you talking about? 'Our baby'? How can that be? I thought you wanted to help her out."

Kay had to compose herself. She'd already said too much, but she knew in her heart there was no turning back now. "Whether or not I want to help her out is beside the point. She lied to me."

"About what?"

"Apparently, before you two broke up, she took it upon herself to take a parting gift—your sperm! That's what she had me impregnated with. I'm having your baby, and she fully expects me to give it up in seven months."

He just stared at her, looking confused, as if English wasn't his first language. It hurt her to see him in such pain. She knew exactly how he felt.

"And you know this is my child for a fact?"

"She told me herself that this was your child. She saved the last condom you two used together. That night when she told you she was going to the bank, she wasn't talking about a financial institution, she was talking about a sperm bank. She's determined to be tied to you for the rest of her life, and she's using me to make that happen."

"If you are carrying my child, Destanie will never get her hands on him or her. We're going to keep the baby and raise it ourselves. We'll get everyone we know to testify about how she's acted over the past year—the things she's said and done. No judge in his right mind would hand a baby over to her," Finesse said. He couldn't believe the situation he was suddenly in. The woman of his dreams was having his baby and was being forced to give it up to the woman that haunted his nightmares. "Man! Wow! Kay, you laid a lot on me. I don't know what to say."

"How 'bout you say, 'I knew that crazy heifer when'? I'm 'bout ready to kill that damn Destanie."

"Baby, you are pregnant. What can you possibly do?"

"Take me over to Destanie's, and I'll show you."

"I think it is time we both gave her a piece of our minds. She needs to know we will never give up our child!"

He drove out of the parking lot and rushed into traffic.

As they drove toward the home of his ex-girlfriend, Kay explained all that she could. She told him in detail about their fight. She made it seem as if she was carrying the baby because Destanie made her feel guilty about the abortion she claimed Finesse forced her to have. She told him that Destanie hoped to win him back once she had a blood connection to him.

Kay felt only slightly guilty for not telling him that she was only carrying out the sick plan because Destanie had pictures of her having sex with her brother-in-law. She knew when they confronted Destanie, *that* little detail would be revealed, but she'd deal with Finney's reaction then. The key was to keep his anger focused as much as possible on Destanie.

The more Kay talked, the more intently Finesse listened—and the less attention he paid to the road and his driving. He was driving way too fast on the slick road. He caught himself and slowed down several times, only to speed up again and again. The frantic pace of his driving matched the frantic pace of his thoughts as he listened to Kay talk about their situation.

"Babe, slow down," Kay told him as he rounded, too quickly, a highway curve not far from Destanie's home.

The SUV's tires lost traction, and the vehicle started to hydroplane. When Finesse overcorrected, the SUV went airborne, flipping over several times as it fell down a 50-foot precipice. As they reached the bottom of the hill, there was shattered glass . . . a loud boom . . . fire . . . and then nothing.

* * * * * * *

The vehicle's license plate was dislodged when it overturned. Within an hour after the accident, the police were able to trace the license back to Madetra, who had co-signed on a car loan for Kay.

When Madetra arrived at the scene, as she looked over the cliff, it was obvious there was nothing significant left. There was nothing left of Finesse. There was nothing left of Kaylantra. There was nothing left of the baby. There was nothing to bury— no bones, no flesh, nothing.

As she continued to look over the railing and mourn her sister, one of the police officers handed her an envelope. In it were the only items on the scene that hinted of Kaylantra's once-vibrant existence. Madetra opened the envelope and looked through its contents: a few pictures and some miscellaneous receipts.

Madetra stared at the pictures, unable to blink or breath. As she stared at them, something deep within her snapped and she began to cry. She cried at the thought of her twin sister being reduced to nothing but a few racy and pornographic photos and some receipts.

She began to shake as the realization set in that her twin sister—her balance, her better half—was dead, gone; lost to her forever. In that moment, while staring long and hard at the obscene pictures of her blindfolded sister having sex with her husband . . . Madetra became nothing too.

DARRYN

Sixteen cocks in a circle.

How had it come to this? He was a married man. He had once been at the top of his profession. He had been ambitious and successful. A star. A king. Now he was on the floor in a hotel room, on his knees, blowing men for money and rocks. He was a "rock hound," a crack whore desperate for money.

What really did him in was hanging out at that strip club. That's where Darryn got himself hooked on all kinds of things that were bad for him, number one among them, his sister-in-law.

To carry out his shameless, dirty deeds with her, not only did he have to blindfold her, but also he had to wear his own blindfold—a mental one. He made sure he was high every time he was with her. He started by drinking himself into oblivion, and then he started doing weed.

As they got wilder together, he needed something stronger to help him release his inhibitions, to help him forget about how he was betraying his wife by having sex with her twin sister. But now that his sister-in-law was dead and buried with another man's baby in her belly, he didn't care much about anything.

He really loved Kay, and she was gone. Now all Darryn cared about was feeding his "jones"—his five-hundred-dollar-a-day coke habit.

He was trying to do a better job of hiding his drug problem from his wife. Luckily for him, her grief for Kay had her a little distracted, and she seemed to think he was getting better. She really had no idea.

His ass-toe started twitching. Ain't life a bitch?

Black warriors of all shapes and sizes stood before him. Apparently word got around on what he was planning to do. Who knew there were so many down-low men in one place?

The men standing before him waiting to get a nut busted ranged in color from butter-colored brothers to Negroes dark as midnight. Some of the penises were young, some were old. Some were chiseled and hard; some were pencil-thin and soft. Some were like round, stubby sausages; some were crooked, with hooks going in every direction. And still others hung "for days" like big, swollen tree trunks. The one thing they had in common—they each belonged to a man willing to wait his turn for another man to put his mouth on him.

He was going to be a busy somethin'-somethin' for a while. It was going to take more than a minute to blow all this nut. And while there were 16 cocks in the circle, there were 16 other men just stand-

ing around behind them looking and laughing. He
figured by the end of the night he'd get some cheddar out of everyone of them too.

It was a good thing he was charging a hundred a
head. That was $1,600, potentially $3,200 dollars,
for a few hours work. That would keep him "in
rock" for nearly a week. But all the rock in the
world couldn't fill the hole in his heart, nor erase
how pitiful he felt when he thought about his wife,
Madetra, and her dead sister, Kaylantra.

Darryn knew he had to make quick work of
these 16-32 men because he had to meet with his
wife in the hotel's restaurant in three hours. Sadly,
he was broke. He couldn't even pay for his part of
the meal, let alone treat her, even though he was
the one who had done the inviting. He decided
he'd think about that later. And after tenderizing
all the male meat he could stand, he was going to
be real anxious for some trim. He hoped his wife
would be ready and willing to be obedient because
he was planning on throwing a killing on her.

As he moved around the circle on his knees,
sucking off one man after another, Darryn fantasized that he was instead indulging in the plea-
sures of a woman, his dead sister-in-law, to be
exact. That helped him get through it all.

*Kaylantra. Kay. From somewhere deep within—his
empty soul perhaps?—he ached.*

Two hours later, with a mouth full of the taste of
"love custard" and a jaw that was stiff and sore,
Darryn was done. The embarrassment of what he'd
done was too much to bear. Every one of the men
that he'd pleasured left either their cards or phone
numbers.

Sickened by the thought of what had just hap-

pened, Darryn crawled on his hands and knees to
the bathroom, turned on the shower, and crawled
into a ball underneath the showerhead, hoping
for the water's cleansing powers to restore his soul.

After a thorough shower and after he'd used up
a full tube of Colgate and two mini-bottles of Lis-
terine, he was dressed and shining like a brand-
new penny. He was just about to walk out of the
hotel room, when his wife hit him up on his cell.

"Talk to me."

"It's me," Madetra said. "I'm in the hotel restaurant. Where are you?"

"I had to take a leak in one of the upstairs bathrooms. All of the bathrooms downstairs were closed
for cleaning," he lied. "I'll be down in a minute."

"Okay, I'll be counting the minutes," she said
before hanging up.

Yeah, I'll be counting the minutes until you die.

Madetra still couldn't get out of her mind the
pictures she found of her husband having sex with
her sister, and for that he was going to pay—just
like all the others were going to pay.

While she waited in the near-empty restaurant
for her husband, Madetra ordered some red wine.
She took a sip from her drink and watched the
door for Darryn. She was surprised when she saw
him walk past the restaurant and up to the reception desk.

*Was she just imagining things, or had almost every
man in the lobby given him a standing ovation?* Unsure
of what she was thinking, feeling, or seeing, Madetra gulped down her drink and then ordered two
more.

Once the bartender turned his back to her, she
placed some sodium morphate and the date rape

drug, Rohypnol, in one of the drinks, smiling broadly the whole time. The wine and Rohypnol would put her husband to sleep, while the sodium morphate would simulate a heart attack. She had never before gooseballed a drink—but then again she'd never before been filled with such hatred and rage.

As she stirred the drink with her finger, she felt the hands of the man she was about to kill on her shoulders. "Hey," he whispered in her ear, "I've been thinking about you all day."

Hearing Darryn's voice made Madetra's blood run cold. "Backatcha," she said as she faked a smile and turned to greet him. "I ordered this red wine for you."

"Great. I sure could use it." He took the drink and gulped it down in one swallow.

"Baby, I've changed my mind about eating down here. I don't want to. I have a key to one of the bungalows in the back, and I heard that behind it is a secluded indoor pool. I thought you and I could do a little something in the pool and then get some room service. Doesn't that sound nice?"

"It sounds perfect; let's roll," Darryn said as he pulled her out of her seat.

She paid for their drinks, and they left the restaurant.

As she led her victim to his doom, Mad asked, "Hey, I got a question for you. Is it just me, or did all the men in the lobby give you a standing ovation when you rolled through earlier?"

"How much have you had to drink, baby? There was some local TV celebrity in the lobby a while ago. That's what all that clapping was about. Shoot, I wish I could command that kind of attention. Actually, the only attention I want to command tonight is yours." Darryn backed her against a wall and gave her mouth a tongue bath.

"Well, I'm going to give you my undivided attention, I promise, but not here," she said.

They walked through a maze of corridors and eventually found their secluded bungalow. They burst into the room groping desperately at each other.

"You ready to tickle our privates? I've got a hard-on that you would not believe," he whispered in her ear between kisses.

"Shhhh! You know my philosophy—show, don't tell. Let's go do it in the pool. For some reason I want to get wet and wild." Madetra stripped out of her clothes and helped him out of his own. She then led him around the corner to the indoor heated pool located behind their bungalow.

"*You* want to get nasty in public? That's something I'll believe when I see it."

"Okay, be prepared to write *Ripley's Believe it or Not.*" Madetra said as she took a flying leap into the pool.

Darryn watched from the doorway as his lovely wife sloshed around in the water, begging him to join her.

His ass-toe began tingling. Great sex? Trouble?

"Come on in. I have something for you," Madetra teased.

As much as he wanted to, Darryn couldn't move. His vision was suddenly blurry, and he felt hot and sick to his stomach. "I'm not feeling too good. I'm going to lay down," he told her, afraid that pleasuring half of the men in the hotel was finally catching up with him.

"Uh, uh, no, you don't."

Madetra got out of the pool and pulled him in to the water with her. She was determined to get herself some loving, even if it killed him.

She leaned him against the wall of the pool, and before he could stop her, she straddled him and was soon riding his rock-hard penis.

She grabbed the pool's railing on both sides of his head, and with short, hard, even strokes, she moved in slow circles, bouncing her tight body off of his stiff love rod.

The pool's water helped drive her to ecstasy as the soothing waves gently crashed into their hot, writhing bodies. She could hear the smack of their wetness echoing in her ears, and it aroused her.

She came much quicker than she would have liked and kept going for round two. The more she impaled herself with his pleasure pole, the stiffer he became and the more he tried to fight her off.

"Stop, baby! I can't! I gotta stop! I'm not feeling good! I think I need a doctor!" He tried to lift her off of him.

"Shut up and just screw me, Darryn!"

Darryn was usually a sucker for a woman making sexual demands, but tonight he couldn't get into it. He thrashed about and tried even harder to lift his wife off of his shaft, but the harder he tried to remove her, the harder she fought to stay in place. Like a suction cup, her body held on tight.

"We have to stop. I can't breathe . . . really," he said as he clutched at his chest.

"That's the idea," she whispered. "I placed some sodium morphate in your drink earlier. I'm guessing you're having a heart attack right about now, but it will soon be over." Madetra humped him doubly hard and fast for good measure. "And when you're good and dead, I'll scream for help. Everyone will fall all over themselves trying to help me, the young, beautiful, distraught, naked widow whose drug-addicted husband tragically had a heart attack and died during sex."

"Why are you doing this? Why are you trying to kill me?" Darryn asked with a weak voice, struggling for air.

"Are you trying to tell me you honestly have no idea why I want you dead? Maybe it's because I secretly hate you. Game recognizes game, remember? Isn't that what you once told me? You're a drug addict that has refused to get help. You've destroyed our life as we knew it. We were once so happy, and now look at us."

"It's not all my fault."

"I know you aren't trying to blame me for the demise of our marriage; I did everything that I could. At least I wasn't having sex outside of our marriage. Okay, that's a lie, but at least I wasn't sleeping with family."

"You had an affair?"

"Yep. With our travel buddy, Gerald. So we're even. I know you had sex with Kay—I saw the pictures at the scene of her accident. Destanie was blackmailing her. Did you know that? She took pictures of you two having sex together."

Darryn's eyes rolled back in his head, and his breathing became even more labored as Madetra slid up and down on him faster and faster before having another orgasm. Seeing him pitiful, helpless, and weak left her breathless; it turned her on a lot more than she could have ever imagined.

For the first time in a long time, she finally felt like she was the one that had the upper hand . . . the power . . . the control in their marriage.

"I can't believe you're trying to kill me," he wheezed.

"Believe it."

Madetra then came for a third time with an ear-piercing scream. When she was done with him, she climbed off his weak body and dove headfirst into the clear blue water. As she maneuvered her body into a backstroke position, Darryn mustered up what little strength he had and tried to get out of the pool.

Unfortunately for him, Madetra had other plans. "Oh, no. You're not going to steal the satisfaction from me of watching you die," she said. She grabbed him by his neck, her ankles interlocked under his chin, and dragged him backwards under the water. An expert swimmer, she could hold her breath underwater for several minutes—and she did just that.

When she finally came up for air, she let go of his neck, and Darryn's limp body floated to the pool's surface. She climbed out of the pool and watched with pride as her first victim lay floating in the pool face down, inhaling water and blood into his lungs, ass saluting the sky. She'd only just begun. Madetra was a doctor and she knew *exactly* what she had to do to make all the murders seem like natural deaths—so that no one would get suspicious and suspect foul play.

"Only three more to go," Madetra heard a voice whisper from a dark, dead place in her soul.

A few days later, once Madetra placed Darryn's obituary in the newspaper, people from every-where called and came by offering their condo-lences, but none of the calls or well-wishers really stood out until the day of his memorial.

As she watched her husband's body sink lower and lower into the ground during a private, no-frills burial service attended only by her, Madetra noticed someone staring at her from across the way. It was Gerald.

"What are you doing here?" she asked as she walked in the direction of her car.

"I wanted to see how you were doing."

"Don't worry about me, I'm a big girl."

"I wanted to call, but I figured you wouldn't talk to me."

"You would have figured right. Gerald, this is to-tally inappropriate. I thought I made it clear in Las Vegas that I didn't want to see you again."

"But what about me? What if I needed to see you?"

"Well, you've seen me, and now you should go."

"I love you," he said simply.

"Are you kidding? At my husband's burial you're trying to rekindle our affair?"

"Yes-I mean-no-I mean-I just had to see you."

"Look, I've been through a lot over the past year. Heck, in just the last few months, I lost both my sister and my husband. I don't need anyone around me reminding me of my losses, and as a

DAT Club member, that's what you represent—
memories of what I've lost."

"He wasn't worth it. He wasn't worth your grief.
He wasn't worth all the pain and guilt you're walking around with. He was an addict who didn't love
or respect you."

"I know exactly what and who my husband was;
you don't."

"Oh, I know. I was there beside you for a long
while, remember? I know exactly what your husband was too. He was a dope fiend. I know . . . because I was the one supplying him with his drugs.
It started at Lake Tahoe and continued until his
death."

"You're the one that got him addicted? You're
the one that sold him his drugs?"

"Come on, Madetra . . . I know we never talked
about it, but you couldn't have been that blind."

"I guess you're right. A part of me knew. That's
all the more reason for me to stay away from you.
You were his dealer, and his addiction killed him.
So, in a way, you killed my husband. Not only that,
but you ruined my life."

"Losing him was the best thing that could have
ever happened to you."

"No, losing you will be the best thing that could
ever happen to me," Madetra said coolly as she
climbed into her car and drove away.

*"The road of life twists and turns and no two directions are ever the same.
Yet our lessons come from the journey, not the destination."*
~ Don Williams, Jr.

E'AN

When the clock in E'an Shaw's office struck the hour of seven, he looked wistfully at the timepiece hanging on his wall.

Normally at this time, he'd be calling Madetra and making plans to ravage her, but those days were over. Her husband was dead and E'an no longer had any leverage over her to keep her involved in their twisted sexual relationship.

So when the phone rang and Madetra was on the other line, E'an was to put it simply—surprised.

"Hello?"

"E'an, be ready tonight at eight o'clock," Madetra said.

"What did you just say?"

"What, suddenly you're deaf?"

"Your husband is dead, that officially releases you from our naughty tryst."

"Who said I wanted to be released?" Madetra

asked. "I thought we could get together tonight and for a change you could try to not humiliate me. Do you think it would be possible for us to actually have a normal date with regular, normal, tender sex?"

He stared at the nude pictures he'd forced Madetra to take. They were open on his computer desktop. He'd just uploaded them that morning and had been staring at them for thirty minutes.

He was surprised yet thrilled to hear the words coming out of her mouth. Her words threw him off-kilter. She knew she was a mindless phuck, didn't she?

Didn't all mindless phucks know that was all they were? She knew the deal—humiliation and remaining distant was the name of the game for him.

But he was in the mood for something new; always being the one in control had gotten old, so he decided to hear her out.

"What are you suggesting?" he asked.

Glad that he took the bait, Madetra—his mindless phuck for the night—did her best to draw him in.

"I'm suggesting you show you have a heart. Why don't we meet at a restaurant? I can wear a disguise. We can role-play the evening away as sexy strangers. We can have a nice, candlelit dinner, and we can actually talk. You know, get to know each other. Then, we could go back to a nice hotel and take a nice, long, lingering shower or bubble bath. We could then rub each other down with some exotic massage oils, and then we can make love. It would be romantic. I know it sounds silly, but since my husband died, I could use a little tenderness and I'm finding more than ever I crave male companionship."

"That doesn't sound silly at all. Go on," he encouraged her, turned on by the fact that she was now seemingly in control.

"We could make love like normal people do . . . in the glow of candlelight with soft music playing nice and low. I could even feed you fruit, and we could drink champagne. Nothing freaky. Nothing degrading. Just tenderness. And for a change, just love."

She knew she was pouring it on a bit thick with the "just love" business, but she also knew she had to do what she had to do.

"What do you mean by 'just tenderness, just love'?" E'an asked suspiciously.

"Open your eyes, silly. Sad and twisted though it may be, you're the one constant in my life, especially now that my husband, Darryn is dead, and it's only natural that I'd develop feelings for you."

"Cut the crap, Madetra. Are you trying to say you love me?"

"No, but the truth is, to quote that popular gay cowboy movie, Brokeback Mountain, 'I can't quit you.' Aren't you tired of meaningless, mindless phuck sex? I know I am. I'm open to other possibilities with you. I want more, possibly love. Do you think you could ever allow yourself to fall in love? Do you think you could even ever fall in like? Why not try it, starting with tonight? I'll bring the champagne, chocolate, and strawberries. You just bring you—and make sure you bring your heart."

"I can't believe you're going to let things between us continue given our past."

"I don't want to be alone much now. It gives me too much time to think about losing Kay and Darryn. Just don't make me regret my decision to continue my involvement with you. Some things are definitely going to have to change."

"Okay, I'm game," E'an said. "I'll meet you at eight. We'll have a normal date. Would that please you?" He stared at his desktop of a close-up image of Madetra's glistening, wet, inner sanctum, which immediately got him rock-hard.

"More than you know."

"Good."

"Yep, I will be," Madetra promised. "I hope you're ready for me, because tonight I'm going to spoil you rotten, E'an. I'm going to kill you with kindness. See you tonight," she said before hanging up.

For E'an, having women at his beck and call had become boring. Every woman who knew him wanted him—he was a prize, a real catch—because after all, he was a rich, attractive doctor. Heck, he'd date himself, if he could.

He'd had plenty of women casually, but no matter how fine they were and no matter how much sex they had, something was missing. Could it be that for once in a long time he actually wanted to feel connected to someone of the feminine persuasion? Could it be he was capable of deeper feelings? Could it be that for once he wanted a soul-to-soul connection with someone else?

As he considered the possibilities of what really could be with a woman, a smile settled on his face and caring crept into his eyes.

" 'Tenderness and just love,' " huh?

* * *

The nice candlelight dinner that Madetra and E'an had talked about over the phone turned out perfectly. When she met E'an at Claudio's Italian Ristorante, she was wearing a short, brown wig, light green contacts and a pair of shoes with very high heels. She looked like a goddess in a strapless, nearly see-through black dress that clung to her curves and made her look shapelier and heavier than she really was.

As the night progressed, Madetra noticed that the men in the restaurant were having a hard time keeping their eyes off her. That could prove problematic.

After their two-hour long dinner, Madetra followed E'an in her car to the nicest Ritz Carlton Hotel in town, where E'an had a standing reservation. As was their normal routine, E'an checked into the hotel, and Madetra snuck up to their room a few minutes later. Once they were settled in the room, she stripped out of her clothes and ran them a hot bubble bath. She lit vanilla candles and placed them around the bathroom's Jacuzzi tub. She then climbed in. After stumbling out of his clothes, E'an soon joined her.

They spent an hour in the tub relaxing, chatting, and laughing, with him lying comfortably between her legs, his head on her chest. After cleansing each other, they climbed out of the tub and toweled each other off.

Madetra lead him seductively by the hand to the room's super large, four-poster bed. She watched as he climbed onto the bed. She then climbed on top of him.

She poured some vanilla massage oil onto her palms and rubbed her palms together before lavishing her body with oil. She then did the same to him.

As she kneaded and rubbed his body from head to toe, she could feel his muscles loosen up underneath her expert touch.

"See, isn't this much nicer than a mindless screw? Isn't this much better than what we've been doing?"

"I wouldn't knock what we've been doing," E'an said with a laugh.

"Of course you wouldn't, but if you knew anything about women—or at least this woman—you'd know that I need to be romanced. But I'm a firm believer in the notion that you get what you give. So, to get romance, I've got to give it. Now you just lay down, and I'll be back in a minute with a few tasty treats."

"The only tasty treat I need is you," he said as he grabbed for her waist.

Always ready for whatever he threw at her, Madetra easily slid between his fingertips. "I won't be gone long, I promise."

Madetra walked casually to the hotel's built-in kitchen and washed the excess massage oil off her hands. She then chopped large juicy strawberries into smaller, bite-sized portions. Then she poured them both a glass of champagne and prepared a chocolate concoction made of rich, expensive chocolate, dioxin, sugar, and arsenic, which she was going to use to dip the strawberries in—a concoction to die for.

She placed all the items on an ornate silver tray lying nearby and then slowly walked back to the poster bed, where a totally relaxed E'an lay.

"So what's your pleasure?" she asked seductively as she stood beside the bed and placed the tray on a nearby nightstand. "Would you like your strawberries first, or would you like a bit of champagne? If it helps with your decision, the champagne is chilled and will be served directly from my body." She poured champagne from one of the glasses down the front of her body.

E'an watched in fascination as the pink liquid rolled over her breasts and cascaded down the length of her body. He could never get enough of her. Eager to taste her, he pulled her onto the bed and hungrily lapped up every drop of the champagne from her breasts, her neck, her stomach, and other parts of her anatomy.

"Wow! Someone is thirsty," Madetra teased.

"Not really. I'm more hungry than anything," E'an growled. Madetra watched with disinterest as his head slowly delved lower and lower down her body.

Just as his mouth was gently probing her mound and inner thighs, he teased her by stopping. "Now how about some strawberries?"

"No one likes a tease," she said, barely able to hide her disgust.

"Let me make it up to you. Let me feed you some chocolate-dipped strawberries," he suggested.

"Nope. I'm supposed to be romancing you, remember?"

How could he forget?

She straddled him and slowly began rocking his member. The barely audible sound of her moaning was music to his ears as he slid in and out of her wet, chocolatey goodness, her moist and gooey center.

He closed his eyes and kneaded her nipples with his hands as she dipped one of the strawberries into the nearby chocolate. "Open wide and give me all of that tongue."

She watched with pleasure as he opened his mouth. She slid the chocolate-dipped strawberry onto his thick, long, pink tongue and watched as his mouth enveloped it.

"Kiss me," he demanded.

"I will, once you eat all the strawberries," she told him. "And if you're a really, really, really, good boy, I'll lick all the excess chocolate off of those luscious lips of yours when you're done."

"Wow! Bring it." He closed his eyes, palmed her hips and burrowed himself deeper inside her moistness.

"Do you really think you can handle much more?"

"I can handle whatever you got," he answered, matching her breathless tone.

"All right, just remember you said that." Madetra dipped two strawberries in the chocolate and then fed them to him, along with her body, smiling deviously all the while.

Within the hour, she'd fed him a half-bushel of strawberries, a quart of her special chocolate concoction, and they had both cum twice.

During her first killing, thanks to her husband, she'd pleasantly discovered there was nothing in the world better than hot, dying dick. But instead of kissing E'an and licking the chocolate from his lips like she promised, Madetra feigned ill and rushed to the bathroom.

After making a few retching noises, she flushed the toilet and came out of the bathroom fully dressed.

"What are you doing with all your clothes on?" E'an asked when he saw her.

"Didn't you hear me throwing up? I don't feel well. I'm going to go home and lay down."

"There is plenty of room in this big, old bed beside me."

"There's been a bug going around at the clinic, and I don't want to infect you—that is if I haven't already done so."

She headed for the door.

"Okay, wait. Let me get dressed. I'll walk you down to your car. Do you even think you'll be able to drive yourself home?"

"Don't worry about me. I can get home fine. You just enjoy the room tonight, and I'll see you at work tomorrow . . . if I'm feeling better. Bye," she said as she slipped out the door before he could say another word.

Madetra had no intention of hanging around and watching E'an suffer through the night from back pain, acute pancreatitis, and nerve paralysis. And just as sure as she knew her own name, she knew the next time she saw E'an Shaw, he'd look a helluva lot different—he'd be laying in a coffin, dead from poisoning, with a badly disfigured face that would be bloated and full of pockmarks, if not partially eaten away.

"And then there were two," she proudly whispered while walking quickly down the hall.

DESTANIE

A week later, unable to concentrate on the news story she was supposed to be writing, Destanie was filled with relief when her ringing cell phone interrupted her thoughts.

"Destanie, it's Madetra from the travel club. Can you let me in? I'm at the back studio door," she heard through her phone's earpiece.

"Madetra? What are you doing here? Uhmmm . . . hold on. I'll be down in a sec."

Destanie walked quickly but with a bit of apprehension down the hallway and down the back stairs. When she finally ushered open the back studio door, Madetra stood in front of her with her face and body hidden under a heavy wool coat and cashmere scarf and hat. "It's freezing out. Thanks for letting me in. Are you surprised to see me?"

"Yeah, I am. Wow! It's been a minute. How have you been?" Destanie gave Madetra an awkward hug. "I wanted to call you after I heard about the deaths of Darryn, Kay, Finesse and E'an, but since you disbanded DAT Club, I wasn't sure if you would want to hear from me."

"The last few months have been tough. Can we go somewhere private and talk?"

Destanie didn't really want to talk, but since Madetra seemed to be really hurting, how could she say no? "Sure. Come on back to my office."

They walked in silence back to Destanie's working corner of the world. "Here, sit down." She pointed to two seats in front of her desk.

Once Madetra sat down, Destanie sat down beside her.

In a whispered, frantic voice, Madetra said, "What I'm about to say may sound crazy, but just hear me out. I can't get my mind off of the past year. Kay and my husband are gone, and so is Finesse. DAT Club has broken up, and I'm having a hard time dealing with all of that. I assumed you might be too, you and Gerald."

"I haven't talked to him, but I'm sure everyone is on his mind. Losing people that were so close to all of us is hard. I cry about it every day."

"I'm sure you do cry for Finesse."

"I cry for Kay too, believe it or not. I feel like what happened to them is my fault."

So do I, Madetra thought.

"That's why I wanted to talk to you."

"Okay, so talk."

"This is the part that might sound weird. I miss my husband. I miss my sister. I'm so lonely. I want to feel close to the two of them again, and I thought since we all spent so much time together over the past year, I could feel close again to them through you. And I'm sure you'd like to feel close to Finney again. I think we can really help each other in that way." Madetra grabbed Destanie's hand. "Because of what we've all shared together in the group, I want you to feel close and connected to Finney—through me. That might help you heal; it might help us both heal."

"What are you saying?"

"He loved my sister so much, and her blood runs through my veins. Aren't you curious to know what it was about her that he found so alluring?"

"Madetra, you've lost your mind! Are you saying you want to sleep with me so you can feel connected to your sister and I can feel connected to Finesse?"

"That's exactly what I'm saying. Come on, admit it—you're curious as to what he was drawn to, what kind of spell she had over him. She was my twin, after all. Wouldn't you like to know what he sensed, felt, tasted?"

Madetra took Destanie's hand and placed it on her breast.

Destanie half-heartedly tried to snatch it back, but from the look in her eyes, it was obvious that she was more than a little bit curious. "I've never been with a woman before," she whispered.

"I'm not just any woman. For you, tonight, I'm Kay . . . your lover's lover."

As if in a trance, Destanie, slowly started to rub Madetra's nipple and to Mad's surprise she felt it quickly become rock hard. She felt herself getting aroused and she loved the feeling. Her breasts were like an on/off switch to her sexuality, and before she knew what hit her, she was on.

Fixated, Destanie stared at Mad's breast. She

rubbed it harder and then grabbed for the other one, cupping them in both hands and rubbing the nipples intensely with her thumbs.

Madetra whimpered as she felt her chocolate nipples rise and harden against the soft silk material of her blouse. She had never been with a woman before either. Her dead husband, Darryn, once tried to get her involved in a threesome back in college, but when the strange woman started to kiss her as he watched, Madetra ran from the room.

But Madetra wasn't running this time. The spirit of her dead sister, Kay, kept her in place and focused.

Ever since that first woman-to-woman kiss in college, Mad had fantasized, off and on, about being with a woman. The thought of getting something she'd wanted a long time—namely both trim and revenge—stoked her. She went in for the kill. She kissed Destanie lightly on the mouth and was pleased when she kissed her back hungrily.

Destanie's tongue dove deeper and deeper in and out of Madetra's mouth. "I wonder if we're kissing like they kissed," Destanie huskily asked when she came up for air.

Madetra could barely speak as she felt her love pot start to drip and boil over. Eager to feed her wicked craving, she moaned and started kissing Destanie again—this time harder and with more passion. Their moans grew loud as their tongues explored the crevices of each other's mouths. To Destanie, Madetra tasted sweet, and she grew more and more excited as she wondered how the rest of her felt and tasted. She started to unbutton her blouse.

Madetra stopped her. "Can we go somewhere a little more private? I'm kind of loud."

"So am I." Destanie giggled. Like a child excited about the prospect of leading someone to her favorite hiding place, Destanie stood up, grabbed Madetra's coat, hat, purse, and scarf, and guided her deep into the bowels of the station. They passed tons of cubicles and rows upon rows of the station's heavy floor-to-ceiling equipment. They eventually walked down a long corridor past five empty editing bays and settled in the very last one at the far north end of the building.

"It's late, no one will come back here," Destanie said as if sharing a secret with her best friend.

They entered a small room that had editing equipment on one side and an overstuffed coach on the other.

"Are you sure we won't get caught?"

"I'm positive. These editing rooms are rarely used. Everyone uses the ones up front. And if someone does come back here, it's kind of understood what's going on in here in this last editing room, if the door is locked and the music is up. Me and Finney spent a lot of time back here," Destanie said with a nervous laugh. She hit a few buttons on the editing equipment and Raheem DeVaughn's song, "Ask Yourself," filled the room.

"I want to make one thing clear—I'm not a lesbian, but I really, really miss being with Finesse. And I'm so curious about why he loved your sister more than me. Is that weird? Is it weird for me to want to be with you for that reason?"

In more ways than you know, Madetra thought.

"I used to wonder all the time about what they

did to each other," Destanie said in a soft, child-like voice that could barely be heard over the music. "Finesse had a voracious sexual appetite; we both did."

"I'm sure they did everything. Just like what I'm going to do to you." Madetra kissed Destanie, grabbed her behind, and grinded hard into her all at the same time.

Before long, warm tears were falling from Destanie's eyes.

"If this is too emotional for you, maybe we should stop," Mad said, pulling away.

"No. I need to feel close to him; I can do that through you. Please don't stop. But let me go first. I want to taste you and see what it was about your twin sister that had him so gone, so mesmerized."

Glad to oblige, Madetra shimmied out of her clothes and walked over to the couch, where she sat down with her legs wide open. Her body looked exquisite as the moonlight hit it through the window behind the couch. Destanie followed suit. She stripped down to nothing and then, as if in a trance, she followed Madetra to the couch.

As Madetra watched her walk toward her, the lower half of Mad's body immediately began to throb, as if it had a heartbeat of its own. Madetra had seen hundreds of female bodies over the years, and Destanie's was by far one of the finest she'd ever seen. She was a little chunky, but she was fiiiine. Madetra couldn't take her eyes off Destanie's body even if she wanted to.

"You like?" Destanie asked as she kneeled before Madetra.

Before Madetra could answer, Destanie's mouth was hungrily stabbing at her aching breasts.

Almost immediately, intense sensations of pleasure began shooting through all parts of her body as Destanie's teeth and tongue grazed both of her big, ripe, cocoa-brown breasts. Destanie's hot, soft, damp flesh against her own and the moisture from Destanie's mouth made Madetra's body come alive in ways her husband didn't. And then when Destanie straddled her and stuck two, then three fingers deep inside of her, moving them in and out at a frantic pace over and over again, an undeniable heat and passion rose in Madetra, which quickly exited her body in the form of a creamy, wet orgasm that surprised them both.

"Wow! Someone climaxes fast," Destanie said with a broad smile as she licked Mad's juices off of her fingers and climbed down out of her lap. She then prepared to have a great deal of fun licking Madetra clean. She bent her face down to Mad's womanhood and tickled her clit with the tip of her tongue. She suddenly became greedy, intoxicated by the power of Mad's punanny, and hungrily supped for nearly thirty minutes from between her legs.

Again, waves of passion rose within Madetra, and she came another two times. Spent, and on a sexual high, Madetra could hardly catch her breath or open her eyes as Destanie laid her head in her lap.

"I wonder if that's what he smelled, how he felt, what he tasted when he was with your sister," Destanie said more to herself than to Madetra.

Who cares? Madetra rolled her eyes. "Your turn," she managed to get out.

The two women switched places; Destanie lay back on the couch, and Madetra kneeled before her.

"Are there certain things he did or said that you want me to do or say, you know, so you can feel close to him?" Madetra asked while rhythmically massaging Destanie's upper inner thighs with long, deep, kneading strokes.

"He ate me raw a lot . . . was almost brutal. I loved that rough stuff. And he loved to bring me to orgasm with my "Silver Dolphin." He was rough with that too. He'd stimulate me until I was one long, shivering Silver-D spasm. He was a far cry from 10 inches, and I always thought he was jealous of my dolphin," she said with a laugh.

"Well, it's not going to be rough tonight. Here, let's take a little something, so we can both relax and go a lot longer." Madetra kissed Destanie on the lips and then reached for an empty syringe in her purse.

Destanie bristled when she saw the syringe. "What the hell is that?"

"It's just a slight sedative. Like I said, it will help us relax."

"I'm not interested in being injected with anything."

"I'm a doctor, remember. It's totally safe. Watch— I'll inject myself first, and then I'll do you; you won't feel anything but a slight sting." Madetra pretended to give herself an injection in her vaginal lips. Then she reached into her purse for another syringe filled with some cocaine she'd found among Darryn's things that she had mixed with ricin.

"Madetra . . . I don't know . . . why not shoot me in my arm?"

"It's more potent and gets in the bloodstream quicker if I shoot you this way. Trust me—it's what Finney and Kay did all the time." Before she could protest further, Madetra plunged the syringe into the fatty tissue of Destanie's vagina.

"Wow! That stings a bit. Can you kiss it and make it better?"

"I'd be glad to." Madetra bent her head down and licked the injection spot as well as every other spot imaginable on Destanie's luscious frame.

Within ten minutes, Destanie had an orgasm. Within another ten minutes, she was dead.

As Madetra felt the life slowly escape Destanie's body, she whispered, "Didn't anybody ever tell you that you should just say no to drugs, especially pure, uncut cocaine mixed with ricin? You tortured my sister and her boyfriend for the past year. All they wanted was to love each other, and you made that impossible. Why couldn't you just let him go? Why couldn't you leave well enough alone? What was it about that man that both you and my sister just had to have? Was he really worth blackmailing my sister over? Relationships come and go, but crazy bitches like you just have to have your way. You refused to let go, and now, because of you, five people are dead, and another one is going to die. You happy, skank?"

Consumed with a growing rage, Madetra had to fight herself to keep from kicking Destanie all over the room.

She dressed the upper half of Destanie's body, slid her skirt back on, up to her knees, and placed the syringe in Destanie's hand, to make the injection look self-inflicted. She then threw on her own clothing and grabbed her purse, hat, scarf, and coat.

There was only one more to go.

Madetra stood back and admired her handiwork

with no emotion. Even though she didn't feel any different—it was official.

Mad was mad. She was a homicidal maniac who was fast discovering that there was a thin line between sane and insane. E'an, her second victim, had taught her that much.

With that thought planted firmly in her gray matter, Madetra stuck her head out the door and exited the editing bay to the soulful refrain of Raheem DeVaughn asking, "Have you ever been to Heaven?"

"Every exit is an entry somewhere else."
~ Tom Stoppard

GERALD

A week later, Madetra knocked frantically on Gerald St. John's door. She didn't know quite what she would say, but she knew she had to see him.

Since the first time she had been with him in Jamaica, whenever she inhaled, she could smell his scent, his essence, that signature aroma exclusive to him. It was the smell of crisp winter air. It was the smell of hope, of a better life and better times. The anticipation of seeing him for the first time since her husband's burial made her realize just how much she missed him.

When he finally opened the door, she wasted no time. She kissed him long and deep.

"Hello to you too," Gerald said with a broad smile when she released him.

Out of all of them, Gerald was the only one that she didn't wish dead. She didn't want to kill him, but, like those before him, he had to die. If there was anyone to blame for her situation, it was Gerald. She had to kill the man who sold drugs to her husband, and she had to try to erase all memories of their affair.

She couldn't stop herself. She had come too far. She had to go through with it. She didn't want any remembrances of the past year—she had to erase all signs of DAT Club, and Gerald was the final link.

Gerald lifted her into his arms. "I've missed you so much."

"Not nearly as much as I've missed you." Madetra laid her head against his rock-hard chest. "I can't believe you're being so accepting of me, especially after how I acted when you came to see me at Darryn's burial service."

"I love you. I'll always be accepting of you."

As he carried her upstairs, Madetra closed her eyes to avoid his gaze.

"I've been so worried about you. Every week, I've seen articles in the paper about these mysterious deaths. I can't believe that everyone in DAT Club is dead except for the two of us. Surely that's a sign that we're meant to be together. It's made me think that maybe someone was targeting the group. Do you think that could be? Maybe it's someone connected to your husband, or maybe it's someone—"

"Gerald, please . . . can we not discuss this? All I want to concentrate on tonight is you . . . us. I know the last time we talked, I was less than friendly; I want to make up for that," she said with a bittersweet laugh.

" 'Less than friendly'? Hell, you were brutal. Especially when I told you I sold your husband his drugs. I thought you were going to jump me. But I only sold him the drugs to prove to you that he wasn't worthy of you."

"You're right. I realize where I belong now. You've always done nothing but treasure me."

"I always have and always will," he said, locking eyes with hers.

"You know what? I want tonight to be really special. Like a new beginning. My heart and body are yearning for you so badly, and I want so desperately to feel you beside me, inside me, Gerald."

"Babe, I want that too," he said as he stretched her out on his bed. "Even though it's been a long time since we've been together, I feel real close to you, just like I always have. Just like I did that first night we were together. That was the night I realized I loved you, only I couldn't tell you that."

He sat down on the bed beside her.

"I wished you had told me how you really felt in Jamaica, but I guess it's true about actions speaking louder than words. Your body told me everything I needed to know." Madetra looked sadly into the deep brown pools of his eyes.

"Ditto," he said with a tender smile. "It's funny . . . even after everything, I feel like you're my soul mate; I want you to be my life partner. I know it's a little soon to be talking like that, especially since your husband just died, but I just had to let you know how I felt. I just want to honor, cherish, and love you until my last breath. We've wasted enough time; I don't want to waste any more."

"Gerald, I feel the same as you do. Really, I do. I love who I am when I'm with you. You make me want to be the best me I can be. You make me want to love and give with all my heart and soul until I can't love and give any more."

Unable to fight their growing passion, and fueled by their desire to feed their bodies and souls to one another, they stripped each other out of their clothes.

He straddled her lean, naked body and as he rubbed the tip of his manhood against her hardening clit, he leisurely traced her thick, soft lips with his tongue.

She closed her eyes and gave in to the sensations that were rising up from deep within.

They explored each other's mouths with deep, wet kisses. While tonguing each other with wild abandon, he cupped her breasts in his hands and guided his tongue along her feminine curves— from her mouth, to her neck, to her shoulder, to her soft heavenly mounds.

He planted light, feathery kisses on the tips of her nipples and then gently tugged on them with his tender lips. The heat from his mouth on her areolas, sent a tingling sensation racing through her body. He licked and sucked her breasts at a growing frantic pace—back and forth, from one to the other—until they became two swollen cocoa-brown mounds of yearning.

Thanks to his expert touch, she was whipped into a molten frenzy of desire beneath his immense muscular frame. Her nipples continued to harden as he buried his face deeper and deeper into her softness. He literally made love to her breasts by rubbing, sucking, and licking them, worshipping them as if they were the last pair on earth.

After a short while, her body was on fire and she knew of only one thing that could douse the flame.

Overcome by the growing wetness between her legs, she whispered hoarsely in his ear, "Do me, baby. Take me now. It's yours, so take it. Take it. Take meeeeee!" She spread her legs wide open and invited him in.

Glad to do her sexual bidding, Gerald eased two fingers deep inside her moistness and found her sweet spot. He was quickly rewarded with a wave of juices that surrounded his digits, a testament to the fact that every nerve ending in her body had come alive.

"Ahhh . . . hell yeah. I've missed you, and I've wanted you for so long," Gerald whispered as he shifted his weight and slowly pushed his hardness inside of her.

He stretched himself over her body as his thick member probed her insides. He settled deep into her inner folds, and she wrapped her legs around his lower back. His hard, aroused rod slowly worked its way in and out of her waiting, wanting melting pot, and each of his deep, forceful thrusts was rewarded with soft, whimpering, feminine moans. His throbbing thickness grew as it slid in and out of her wetness at an increasingly feverish pace. He repeatedly stiffened and then slowly melted into her.

When their bodies could take no more, they exploded in unison in an intense orgasmic release. Crying out together in ecstasy, they couldn't deny their soulful connection.

As if their bodies had minds of their own, for the next several hours they loved each other again and again in every way imaginable, until both of their bodies were sore, exhausted, and spent.

While she meant what she'd said earlier, Madetra was torn about her feelings for Gerald. She loved him at one time, and a part of her still did. But a part of her also despised him. He was in large part responsible for her dead husband's growing drug addiction, and for that she could never forgive him.

In the afterglow of their lovemaking, as they lay in each other's arms gently caressing one another, Madetra nearly confessed several times to the DAT Club murders she'd committed—including his.

Within twenty minutes, Gerald was asleep.

As he slept, Madetra crept down to the living room and pulled a peanut butter sandwich out of her purse. She ate the sandwich quickly and then popped a half box of cinnamon Altoids into her mouth to mask the taste and scent. When she was done, she stealthily returned to Gerald's bedroom and stirred him awake with a deep and soulful kiss.

As she kissed him, she imagined what the severe allergic reaction would do to his body after he went into anaphylactic shock.

Peanut allergies could be deadly—the swollen windpipe which would eventually block his airways and stop his breathing, the hives, the plunging blood pressure, the cramps and nausea, increased heart rate, vomiting, diarrhea, and swelling of the face, throat, lips, and tongue. It wouldn't be pretty, and without shots of cortisone and epinephrine, otherwise known as adrenaline, he'd suffer.

Madetra sighed and kissed him deeper. Gerald mistook her sigh for passion and drew her closer to him.

In another life, she really could have loved him— before her sister's death, before her mental break, and before she murdered her husband, E'an, and Destanie.

She needed desperately to erase all the bad memories and pain that the last year represented. Gerald had to die because of his open disdain for her marriage and her life as she knew it; her husband had to die because of his drug addiction and his affair with her sister; E'an had to die because of his sexual blackmail; and Destanie had to die because of the way she'd treated Madetra's dead sister, Kay.

As she continued to kiss Gerald passionately, Madetra knew it wouldn't be long before his peanut allergy took effect. She noticed almost immediately that he seemed to have a problem with his breathing—that spurred her on to kiss him harder and deeper.

As his windpipe continued to swell and close up, she noticed that hives were starting to bubble up all over his body. He started gagging, and his breathing became even more labored.

After suffering for nearly ten minutes, Gerald St. John finally took his last breath and died in Madetra's arms.

"It is done," she whispered aloud.

For Madetra, it was finally over.

About Michelle Buckley

Trippin' is Michelle Buckley's second novel. Released by Carl Weber's Urban Books, it originally hit bookshelves in July 2006 and was re-released in May 2008. It was named the Best General Fiction Novel for 2006 by Blackrefer.com, a popular African-American website.

Michelle's first novel, *Bulletproof Soul*, was released in May 2005. As a result of her debut writing effort, *Black Issues Book Review Magazine* included her in the July/August 2005 issue as an up and coming African American author—a "fresh breeze." Also during the summer of 2005, *Bulletproof Soul,* was selected as a *Vibe* book of the month and a *Blackexpressions.com* *"Editor's Pick"* and *"Summer Favorite."*

Michelle is also a featured essayist in the Essence #1 best-seller, *Souls of My Sisters*—a collection of true life essays written by black women for black women, released in 2000 by Kensington's Dafina.

* * *

A journalist by trade, Michelle has written for publications like *Black Enterprise Magazine* and the *Kansas City Business Journal*. She currently lives in Kansas City where she runs her own public relations firm, Perfect Pitch Communications.

To learn more, please visit Michelle Buckley online at *www.michellebuckley.com,* *www.michellebuckleyblog.blogspot.com* or *www.myspace.com/michelle_buckley.*

A Reading Group Guide

Discussion Questions

Trippin'

By Michelle Buckley

About this Guide:

The suggested following questions are intended to enhance your reading and enjoyment of Michelle Buckley's novel, Trippin'.

Reading Guide for Trippin'

1. For a long while Madetra denies her feelings for one of the members of DAT CLUB. Beyond the obvious reason, why do think that is? Why do you think she eventually submits to her feelings and just as quickly has a change of heart?

2. Examine the main characters and their development. Some grow. Some don't. Which ones change for the better? Which ones change for the worse? Which don't change at all? Who was your favorite character? Your least favorite?

3. Stalking is a major issues covered in this book. Is there a fine line between simply being curious and interested in someone and stalking them? Can it really be considered love if the pursuing party practices acts of repeated deceit and trickery? Have you or someone you've known ever stalked or been stalked by someone else?

4. Several people in this novel find themselves doing things that are out of character for them. One in particular turns to life on the down low and murder. When life throws you unexpected curve balls, how do you handle them? What keeps you from doing things that are "out of character" for you? How could the characters in the book have dealt with their less than ideal situations more effectively?

5. If you could travel anywhere—where would you go and why?

6. When it comes to addictions—drugs, sex, etc.—how did the novel's characters and the people close to them deal (or not deal) with the addictions?

7. The issue of surrogacy is an important one in this novel. If you were asked to carry a child for someone else, would you do it? If so, under what circumstances?

8. Murders both planned and accidental take place in the novel. Examine the killers' mind-sets before their heinous acts. If you could murder someone and get away with it, how would you do it?

9. Sexuality on the Internet from live webcam viewings to porn sites, group chats and every-thing in-between is pervasive. Some call it safe sex. Others think it's the Devil's sexual playground. What do you think about the var-ious forms of sex on the 'Net and how it's af-fecting society as a whole?

10. How is the issue of sexual harassment in the workplace dealt with? Have you been sexually harassed at work or do you know of someone who has? How did the situation turn out? Do you think this issue is more prevalent in the workplace than we realize?